Chapter One

"So you're the best ForeverLove.com has to offer." The silky male voice seemed to engulf Alexis Graham the moment she walked through the imposing double mahogany doors into the executive suite of Grady McCabe Enterprises.

"And you must be Mr. McCabe," Alexis replied, striding forward and holding out her hand. Although why the eldest son of the legendary Josie and Wade McCabe would need to hire a matchmaking agency was beyond her.

At thirty-five, the wildly successful Texan was renowned for the skyscrapers he built and leased to businesses throughout the Southwest. He was no slouch in the looks department, either. Six foot four inches tall, with the kick-butt physique of a Hollywood heartthrob, he had a strikingly masculine face that commanded attention. He wore his dark brown hair in a short, sexy cut that looked great even now in rumpled disarray. His tie was loosened, the first two buttons undone, and the sleeves on his pale blue dress shirt were rolled up to his elbows, revealing strong, sinewy forearms. As he moved, Alexis couldn't help but notice his flat stomach and lean hips.

His lips curved upward. "Call me Grady." He clasped her hand in his big, rough palm. "And let's get right to it, shall we?"

Her skin still tingling from his brief, warm touch, Alexis sat down and removed a notepad and pen from her leather briefcase.

Grady circled his desk and sat down in his high-backed leather chair. "I need a mommy for my five-year-old daughter, Savannah, and I'm willing to marry to get one."

Alexis made a note of that, before gazing up into his deep velvet, blue eyes. "I have to tell you—that's not the best opening for a man on a first date."

Grady McCabe obviously couldn't have cared less. "I'm not going to be less than honest," he told her bluntly. "Which is where you come in."

Alexis was beginning not to like this. Or at least not like the commercial real estate developer's attitude. She had gotten in the matchmaking business because she believed wholeheartedly in the possibility of lifelong love. She knew how short life was, how cruel fate could be, and she wanted to be instrumental in helping well-meaning couples find each other. But what she did *not* want to do was promote loveless unions. Unfortunately, her employers were not as idealistic. The four business partners who owned ForeverLove.com only cared that the customers left happy, and the bottom line remained healthy.

Grady McCabe was an important client. Not only was the multimillionaire a member of the famed McCabe clan of Laramie, Texas, he was one of the premiere businessmen in Fort Worth. His mixed-use development projects were the pride of the downtown area.

Alexis had been given the task of ensuring that Grady found whatever he wanted in a woman, no matter what it took. A lot was riding on her success.

Grady sent her a level look. He seemed to know that what

he was asking was highly unusual. That made him no less serious in his ambition, however.

"I already had the best. I lost my wife shortly after our daughter was born. A few days after we took the baby home from the hospital, Tabitha had an aneurysm and cerebral hemorrhage that resulted in her death."

Alexis recalled reading about it in the paper. Grady had been at work and had come home to find his wife, but by then it was too late. The funeral had brought many prominent people to Fort Worth. Grady's grief, the tragedy of a young mother dying so suddenly and the newborn baby growing up without a mother, had been all folks talked about for weeks. "I'm sorry."

Grady accepted Alexis's sympathy with a grim nod. "Since then I've had nannies. A lot of them, actually. My eighth one just quit."

"Goodness," Alexis murmured before she could stop herself.

Grady kicked back in his chair with a heavy sigh. "I'm not surprised. Savannah doesn't need a nanny. She needs a mother." He paused to give Alexis a pointed look. "Which is where you come in."

Alexis did not deny Grady needed help, when it came to the domestic front. "I'm supposed to find women for you to date and hopefully marry."

He shook his head. "You are supposed to find a woman who will make a great mommy for Savannah."

It was Alexis's turn to disagree. "That's not really what we do at ForeverLove.com."

"I've spoken to your boss, Holly Anne Kirkland, and she assures me that not only will it be done, but you are the right person to do it." Grady's blue eyes narrowed in obvious displeasure. "Was she wrong?"

THAT SHOULD HAVE BEEN an easy question, Grady thought. One that brought forth a flurry of apologies and assurances that yes, his demands would be met, without any further delay.

Instead, Alexis Graham studied him in thoughtful silence.

He couldn't say he minded. The pause in conversation gave him a chance to size her up, too. Decide if she was indeed the right woman for the task.

Outwardly, she certainly looked it.

The thirty-something matchmaker had the city-chic sophistication of the upwardly mobile career woman she was reputed to be. Her figure-hugging suit was made of a pale yellow fabric perfect for the balmy June weather. Understated makeup accented the delicate, feminine features on her oval face, drawing attention to her high cheekbones, soft full lips and long-lashed, teal-blue eyes. Her shoulder length, honey-blond hair only added to the aura of pulled-together perfection. Had he been in the market for a dalliance with an intelligent, engaging female, he would have had to look no further. He wasn't.

All he wanted was a solution to his problem.

And the sooner Alexis Graham understood that, the better.

"Should I ask for another matchmaker from the agency?" Grady drawled.

"No. Of course not." Alexis exhaled sharply. "I've been assigned the job. I'll do it."

"Good, then let me tell you what I want."

She picked up her pen and notebook and began to write, but Grady couldn't help but notice her exasperation.

"First and foremost, my daughter has to like this woman. She has to be the mommy of Savannah's dreams."

"What does Savannah want?" Alexis inquired coolly.

If Grady had a clue about that, he wouldn't be in this position. "You'll have to ask her." His little girl was not cooperating with him on any level right now, for reasons known only to her.

With no discernible change in her expression, Alexis continued taking notes.

Grady added even more seriously, "Second, and equally important, the candidates you present to us will have to understand a marriage to me will be in name only. There will be no romance, no sex, no emotional intimacy—other than the normal family dynamic. There, I can promise everything will be status quo."

The elegant arch of Alexis's blond brows lifted slightly.

"You have a problem with that?" he asked.

"I don't think any woman in her right mind will agree to that. Unless..." faint color tinged Alexis's cheeks "...you're giving your potential mate license to look elsewhere for, um...companionship?"

Grady frowned. "Absolutely not. Any woman who marries me will have to be completely faithful to me and our family. Otherwise, it would be too confusing for Savannah."

Alexis sighed. "So this woman is just supposed to do without sex and romance for the rest of her life?"

Her sarcasm grated on his nerves. "It's not impossible." He had been doing without both since his wife died and had been managing okay. "Particularly when one trades that for the love of a family and a luxurious lifestyle." He paused, discerning that Alexis was still not convinced. "I am sure there are women who get that," he said dryly.

She nodded and scribbled something else. "Oh, I have no doubt that you're right."

"Then..." he prodded.

Looking reluctant to speak her piece, but also determined, Alexis sat back in her chair and eyed him carefully. "If I may?"

Grady had a feeling he was going to regret this, but not knowing what was on the tip of her tongue would be worse. "Go ahead."

She lifted her slender shoulders in a shrug. "I think you're selling yourself short. It's not just the woman who deserves more, Grady. You do, too."

"SO HOW DID IT GO?" Holly Anne asked when Alexis returned to the penthouse offices in downtown Fort Worth.

Alexis looked at the managing partner. The forty-year-old entrepreneur had founded the matchmaking business fifteen years prior. Of the four investing partners, she was the only one involved in the day-to-day operations. The others came and went as the demands of their other business ventures allowed.

Holly Anne was the one who delivered the sales pitch that brought in all the wealthiest clients. She was also a pretty tough taskmaster, expecting nothing less than absolute devotion from the firm's twenty-seven employees. Alexis figured her boss had thought long and hard about whom she was going to send to see Grady McCabe.

Alexis followed her into her office. "You knew what he was going to ask me to do, didn't you?"

Her boss ran a hand through her sleek black bob, paused to adjust one of her diamond earrings, and sank down in her custom leather chair. "He might have mentioned his request was unusual."

Alexis looked past her toward the view of the skyline. Without warning, she could feel a hint of melancholy coming over her. She pushed it away and began to pace. "Unusual or ridiculously heartless?"

Holly Anne gestured for her to sit down. "He has a lot of money."

Reluctantly, Alexis complied, crossing her legs at the knee. "Not to mention the McCabe name."

"The family is legendary," Holly Anne agreed.

And notoriously warm and loving, Alexis had heard, wishing she could be part of such a large, inclusive clan. Unfortunately, she'd been an only child and had lost both her parents in a car accident. She sighed and let loose some of her pent-up emotion. "Which makes me wonder if they know what he's up to."

Holly Anne tilted her head to one side. "I imagine they want to see him married again."

"Not this way."

"Maybe any way. He was completely in love with his late wife."

Alexis knew how that felt. She had been completely in love with her late spouse, too. She swallowed, then forced her mind back to the present, and the ethical problem in front of her. "So he said."

Her boss paused again. "I chose you, Alexis, because I thought you would understand where Grady is coming from, better than anyone else on staff."

She did, Alexis thought, as silence fell. And she didn't….

Holly Anne leaned forward, a compassionate gleam in her eyes. "I know this is an unusually tough assignment, but you're the right matchmaker for the job. Unless…your heart isn't in this anymore?"

Lately, Alexis had been wondering that herself. Had she been doing this way too long? Not always for the most idealistic of reasons? Or was she just feeling blue as she always did when the second weekend of June approached and she was forced to confront all those painful memories? She turned back to her boss. "Is that what you think? That I'm burned out?"

"I think you've been on track for a promotion for many years. Finding that perfect woman for Grady McCabe would not only make his little girl very happy, but it would put you at the top of the list to run the new office in Galveston." Holly Anne paused. "The move to the coast would be a fresh start for you. And the bump up in salary is considerable."

And money, Alexis thought, was essential if she ever wanted to get out of debt, put the past behind her and live in something more than a tiny efficiency apartment in a not-so-great neighborhood. And Holly was right. In the middle of this crazy request was a little girl who'd never really known her mother, and wanted—as every child did—to have a mommy in her life. If Alexis could find someone who was right for Grady and his daughter, it was possible love could blossom. Grady McCabe could get more than he expected. He could do what she was trying to do right now—come all the way back to life again.

Alexis smiled. "Then I'll do it." And in the process, maybe convince Grady McCabe that it's plain crazy to give up on love.

GRADY WASN'T SURE what had happened in the last month or two to make his daughter so uncooperative where her schoolwork was concerned. He did know that at-home assignments were a stringent part of the curriculum at the prestigious Miss Chilton's Academy for Young Women.

Not that it would take the incredibly bright child very long to actually do the work sheet, if she would just get to it.

Savannah slumped on the leather sofa in his study, the

picture of five-year-old distress. "But Daddy, I don't *want* to do my homework."

Grady worked to curtail his exasperation. "It's not up for discussion, Savannah," he reminded her gently.

"I want to go outside and swing!" she whined loudly.

"*After* you've finished your work sheet," he promised.

Savannah's lower lip slid out, and tears welled in her eyes.

The doorbell rang.

Grady sighed and went to answer it.

Alexis Graham stood on the other side of the portal. She looked every bit as beautiful as she had that afternoon in his office. Briefcase in hand, she was clearly ready to get to work. "Come on in." He stood back to let her pass. "I've got someone I want you to meet."

The only problem was, when he entered his study, his daughter wasn't there. "Savannah," Grady called, and was greeted with silence. "Savannah!" His voice turned stern. He looked behind the sofa, the desk, in the storage closet concealed behind paneled doors.

No sign of her anywhere.

Her abandoned homework sat on the child-size wooden table in the corner, next to her pushed-back chair. Figuring he knew where she had gone, Grady grumbled, "You may have to interview her outside."

Alexis's shapely brow lifted in inquiry.

"Savannah's going to have to approve of anyone I marry," Grady explained, leading the way through the sprawling first floor of his multimillion-dollar home, to the French doors that opened onto the patio. "So I figured we'd start by finding out precisely what she wants in a mother."

As suspected, his misbehaving daughter was seated on her swing, knowing full well that she was doing something wrong. "Look how high I can go, Daddy!" she exclaimed, pumping her legs.

Figuring the lecture could wait, Grady said, "Savannah, this is Ms. Graham. She's going to help us find someone to take care of you."

Savannah's eyes narrowed. "I don't want another nanny!"

"I know you don't." He stopped the swing, then hunkered down in front of her, so the two of them were at eye level. "Which is why we're now looking for a *Mommy.*"

NOT EXACTLY THE WAY Alexis would have put it. But now that the matter-of-fact declaration was out there, she figured they were just going to have to go with it.

"Your daddy," she said, picking up where Grady had left off, "is looking to get married again. His new wife will be your mommy and that's why we want to know what kind of one you want, before I actually start searching."

Savannah McCabe scrunched up her eyes and twisted her mouth thoughtfully. The face she was making did nothing to diminish her prettiness. Grady's five-year-old daughter was incredibly beautiful. A halo of wild honey-blond curls framed her expressive face. She had bright blue eyes and thick, curling lashes. Round cheeks, a pert nose and a pugnacious little chin added to her angelically stubborn aura. She was tall and athletically built—like her daddy—yet feminine, too.

She was dressed in a ridiculously frilly pink organza dress, with mismatched purple-and-yellow-polka-dot tights and lime-green cowgirl boots. A red-and-white striped barrette in the shape of a candy cane had been shoved into her uncombed hair.

She clearly had Grady McCabe wrapped around her little finger.

Although Alexis doubted he saw it that way.

"I don't want a mommy, either," Savannah declared. "I just want my daddy." She hopped down off the swing and pushed herself into his arms.

Grady hugged her close. Over Savannah's head, he met Alexis's eyes.

This, he hadn't expected.

However, Alexis had.

No little girl who'd had her father's undivided attention was going to want an interloper in their lives.

"Sweetie, you know you need a mommy," he was saying.

"My mommy's in heaven."

"That's right. Which is why," Grady continued, "your mommy wants you to have another mommy now. Someone who can be with you and help you do things."

"Like what?"

"Like…go shopping, bake cookies and go to the park—and comb your hair and all that stuff."

"*We* do that." Savannah pushed away from Grady and hopped back on her swing.

He moved back as she began swinging madly, the petulant look again on her face.

Alexis put a hand on Grady's arm before he could say another word. The tensing of his bicep made her fingers tingle. When their glances met, she silently beseeched him to let her handle this.

Dropping her hand, she stepped away from him and turned to Savannah. "Let's pretend that I'm your fairy godmother."

Savannah's eyes widened in interest. "Like in *Cinderella?*"

"Sort of." Alexis smiled. "Only instead of me making you

into a princess, I will help you and your daddy look for a real live princess to come and be your new mommy. What do you think about that?"

"A princess could be my mommy?"

For the kind of lavish lifestyle Grady was offering, Alexis figured he could get anything he wanted from a woman interested in that.

She nodded. "Of course, she would look a lot like everybody else's mommy." She set down her briefcase in the grass and sat in the swing next to Savannah's, nodding at Grady to do the same.

Reluctantly, he took the swing on the other side of his daughter.

Alexis began to swing at the same level and speed as Savannah. "And she'd be kind and loving…and lots of fun."

"Would she play games with me?"

Alexis smiled. "Oh, yes."

"And dress-up?" Savannah pressed.

"Absolutely." Or else she wouldn't be a candidate, Alexis thought.

"And she'd help you with your homework," Grady interjected.

"Then I don't want one," the little girl declared. "Because I don't want to do my homework ever again!" That said, she hopped out of the swing and stomped inside the house.

Alexis offered a sympathetic smile. "Do you want to go after her?"

He shook his head. "I'll give her a few minutes to cool off first."

She couldn't help but feel bad for the man. He obviously loved his daughter very much, but was at a loss as to how to handle her. At times like this, another parent would come in handy. "I gather homework is an issue?"

"Recently, yes, for no reason any of us can figure out. Savannah knows how to write all her letters and numbers and color in the lines, and she does those things without a problem at school." He shrugged helplessly. "She just doesn't want to do them at home."

"You've talked to her teacher?"

"She can't understand Savannah's increasingly recalcitrant behavior either, but it's to the point now that if Savannah doesn't perform as required, they're going to have to hold her back a year. I don't want that to happen," he said emphatically. "I think she's more than ready for first grade, intellectually. Emotionally, well, I think not having a mother is beginning to be an issue for her. So I'm hoping that if I solve that problem, I'll solve the homework problem."

Feeling as if they were finally getting somewhere, Alexis guessed, "Which is why you decided to get married ASAP."

Grady nodded with determination. "I'd like to be married by the Fourth of July."

Once again, Alexis was knocked off-kilter by his demands. "Why so fast?"

"Savannah's in a year-round school program. She graduates from kindergarten on June thirtieth and then is off until first grade starts on August first. I think it would be helpful to her to spend the month of vacation getting to know her new mother."

Alexis understood that Grady was used to getting things done quickly, in business. "You don't want to work that fast," she warned. There was no possible way they could find a suitable wife in less than a month!

His jaw set. "I think it can be done in that time frame."

She knew the customer was always right. Still, she felt she had to at least try and talk sense into him. "What Savannah needs," she urged gently, "is for you to take as much time as necessary to do this right."

He looked irritated, but at least willing to listen to what she had to say. "Then what would you suggest? How can we do this right and still do it fast?"

Alexis drew a bracing breath. "First, I need to spend time with Savannah. If I'm to find someone who is going to be compatible with you both, I've got to understand a lot more about what the two of you want. And while you certainly can fill out the detailed questionnaires that the agency provides, Savannah can't."

Grady caught her drift. "Want to start by staying for dinner with us tonight?"

He's just a client. Albeit a very handsome one. "Sure." Alexis forced herself to maintain a businesslike attitude. "If that would make it easier."

"A lot, actually."

The French door from the family room flew open and Savannah stomped out. She was wearing a violet feather boa, a red cowgirl hat...and an attitude that begged for some one-on-one attention. "How come you're still out here swinging—when I'm mad?" She planted her hands on her hips and glared at both of them.

Grady seemed to know that what his daughter really needed at that moment was some tender loving care. "We were talking about what to do next," he soothed.

"Your dad asked me to stay for dinner with the two of you," Alexis reported. And in an effort to include Savannah, she added, "Is that all right with you?"

The child lowered her head and dragged the toe of her cowgirl boot across the patio flagstone. "Well…." She drew out the word. Threw up her hands even more dramatically. "Okay. I guess!"

"Great!" Grady winked at Alexis. "I'll throw something on the stove while you girls get to know each other."

Chapter Two

"Close your eyes, Daddy!" Savannah shouted from the hallway just beyond the kitchen. "And don't open them until I tell you to, okay?"

Grady grinned. He didn't know what Alexis and Savannah had been talking about in her bedroom while he'd been preparing dinner, but his little girl sounded a lot happier.

"Okay." After setting the baking tray on top of the stove to cool, he leaned against the counter and closed his eyes. "I'm ready," he shouted back.

"Are you sure your eyes are closed?" Savannah called.

"Yes." To convince her, he put a hand over them. "I can't see anything!"

"Okay!" Savannah exclaimed, "'Cause ready or not, Daddy, here we come!"

This ought to be good, Grady thought.

He heard the familiar clomp of Savannah's cowgirl boots coming down the hardwood hallway. Followed by the tapping of Alexis's high heels.

Seconds later, he felt the movement of bodies, and inhaled the sexy, feminine scent of Alexis Graham's perfume.

Savannah giggled. "Okay, Daddy, you can look now!"

Grady opened his eyes and found his daughter in one of her dress-up costumes. Her cowgirl boots peeked out from beneath the hem, a jeweled crown adorned her head, and the boa encircled her neck.

Beside her, Alexis stood. Her honey-blond hair was swept into an elegant knot, on the back of her head, and she, too, wore a child-size tiara and a great deal of play jewelry. Her regal attire consisted of a makeshift shawl wrapped around her shoulders and a ruffled pink-and-white cotton "skirt" that suspiciously resembled one of Savannah's bedroom curtains.

"We're playing dress-up," Savannah announced. "I'm the princess and Alexis is my fairy godmother!"

"So I see." Grady worked to contain his pleasure before trading glances with Alexis.

She solemnly waved a magic wand at Savannah, and the little girl beamed up at her. To his surprise, Alexis seemed to be enjoying herself every bit as much as his daughter.

"And she said I can call her Alexis if I want!" Savannah declared.

Grady grinned. He wanted his daughter attaching herself emotionally to her new mother, not the woman he had hired to *find* them one.

Alexis met his eyes. Seeming to understand his reservation, she said, "I think it's important if Savannah and I are going to be friends that the two of us be on a first-name basis."

Put that way, Grady decided, it was acceptable to forgo the traditional method of address.

"You can call her Alexis, too, Daddy," Savannah chimed in.

Grady wasn't sure he wanted even that level of intimacy with a woman he found so physically attractive. But if it made his daughter happy… And Savannah did look happier than he had seen her look in a very long time. "Then I will," he agreed with a smile.

"And you know what else?" Savannah babbled as she sat down in her chair at the breakfast room table, her poufy skirt fluffing out around her. "Alexis is going to find me the kind of mommy I always wanted to have, and she's going to do it right away! Isn't that awesome?"

"It is awesome." Surprised that Alexis had been able to change Savannah's mind so easily, Grady put dinner on the table. Breaded fish sticks from the freezer, macaroni and cheese out of a box, creamed corn from a can and applesauce from a jar.

If Alexis was surprised at the pedestrian fare, she didn't show it.

Grady checked to make sure they had everything, and realized he had forgotten the tartar sauce and ketchup.

He got both from the fridge.

"Do you want anything else for your fish sticks?" he asked Alexis.

Looking impossibly at ease in curtains and a tiara, Alexis spread her napkin across her lap. "Tartar sauce will be fine, thanks. This looks delicious."

Savannah leaned toward her eagerly. "My daddy's a very good cook. He knows how to make all my favorites."

Grady filled her plate, put a puddle of ketchup next to her fish sticks and handed it to her. "So what else have you ladies been doing?" he asked curiously.

"You tell him," Savannah said, her mouth half-full.

Grady gestured to remind Savannah to remember her manners, and Alexis grinned. "We've been trying to figure out what kind of mom a princess would want her fairy godmother to bring her."

"And what kind of mother would that be?" he asked.

Alexis regarded Grady with a deadpan expression. "The kind that likes to read stories and play dress-up and never makes Savannah do her homework."

He worked to suppress a groan. He should have seen that coming. But when it came to his daughter, he was a total push-over.

Alexis responded to Savannah's wordless pantomime and reached over to cut up the fish sticks on the child's plate—something Grady had forgotten to do.

Savannah basked in the extra attention and help, even saying a polite thank-you afterwards.

Alexis added a tiny amount of tartar sauce to her fish. "She should also let Savannah stay up as late as she wishes, and wear whatever she wants to kindergarten. And she should let her eat candy and cake instead of vegetables and fruit. And buy only chocolate milk at the store."

"I can see you've given this a lot of thought," Grady remarked to his daughter.

"And most important of all—" Alexis looked at Grady steadily "—she wants her new mother here in time for her kindergarten graduation. That way she'll have a mommy and a daddy there with her, just like everyone else."

"THANKS FOR STAYING," Grady told Alexis several hours later. The curtain, play jewelry and tiara were gone. One again Alexis was garbed in a sophisticated business suit and heels. Her hair was still in an elegant knot on top of her head, but a few strands had slipped down the nape of her neck. She looked even prettier than she had before.

He pushed the thought away. It was not like him to notice.

That wasn't why she was here, a fact they were both very well aware of.

"Where would you like to talk?" Alexis asked, tilting her face up to his.

"The formal dining room," Grady decided, since it was the closest thing he had to a conference room in his home.

They sat opposite each other. Alexis opened up her briefcase and removed a pen and notepad emblazoned with the company logo and her name. "I don't know about you, but I think we may have made a mistake involving Savannah so closely in the selection process."

"You're referring to her list of desired traits in a mother?"

Alexis nodded, observing him as keenly as she had his daughter. "Savannah now has a very clear picture of what she wants."

Grady stretched his legs out in front of him and slumped back in his chair. "She also knows granting all those wishes is impossible. No parent with the best interest of their child in mind behaves that way."

Alexis was silent. "You and I know that. I'm not so sure Savannah does."

"What are you saying?" Grady prompted.

Alexis cupped her chin in her hand and predicted glumly, "It's going to be tough finding someone by graduation."

Grady shrugged. He refused to lower his expectations just because they had hit a snag. He didn't think Alexis should, either. "I've closed more than one impossible-to-pull-off business deal in less than two weeks."

Her blue eyes darkened. "That's just it," she countered. "This isn't business, Grady. It's personal."

Only to a degree, Grady thought; since he did not plan to get emotionally involved with the woman who would be rearing his child. Had this been anything other than a business arrangement, it *would* have been complicated. "Just go through your files," he advised, not bothering to mask his impatience. "Find some likely candidates. Introduce them to Savannah. And don't make this any more complex for any of us than it has to be."

Alexis tensed. After sending him a look of thinly veiled displeasure, she asked with forced politeness, "Are you certain you don't want to meet them first?"

Grady had vowed when his wife died that he would never love a woman that way again. It was a promise he had kept—and intended to go right on keeping—no matter how much his little girl wanted a mother. "A bit pointless, don't you think, if my daughter doesn't warm to them first?"

Alexis compressed her lips. "I'll be frank. I'm worried she could get hurt."

"She's already been hurt, from the first moment she figured out what a mommy was and learned hers was already in heaven."

The matchmaker's expression turned compassionate. "I need to know what you're looking for, too," she said, writing Grady's name across the top of the page.

Finding it too uncomfortable to look into her eyes, he studied the way her hair gleamed in the light of the chandelier overhead instead, then wished he hadn't noticed. "I already told you my requirements."

She waited in silence until he looked straight at her. "For this to work on even the most rudimentary level, you and Savannah both have to be compatible with the match. So let's start again. What do you want in a woman?"

Grady curbed his temper with effort. "A loving mother for my daughter. An undemanding but understanding wife for me."

“Is she going to need to be able to entertain?”

“Yes.” He folded his arms across his chest.

“Cook?”

He pushed away the too-intimate memory of Alexis having dinner with them in their kitchen. He wondered if she had any idea how hard it was for him to let a woman into his life again, even in theory. How hard it was going to be to open himself up to even the possibility of loss.

Savannah had already lost one mother.

How would they survive if it happened again?

Grady snapped out of his reverie when he realized Alexis was still waiting on an answer to her last question. “I don’t care if she can cook or not. Any woman you bring into our lives is going to have to be able to eat Savannah’s favorite foods with as much gusto as I do, though.”

Finally, the faint hint of a smile tugged at the corners of Alexis’s lips. She wrote “fish sticks, mac’n cheese and applesauce” on the pad in front of her. “What else does Savannah like to eat?”

This, Grady thought, was a lot easier to talk about. “Chicken fingers, hamburgers, hot dogs, grilled cheese, spaghetti, pizza and tacos.”

She kept writing. “That’s it?”

“It’s enough that we don’t have to repeat anything for eight days. And I don’t have to expand my culinary repertoire.”

Alexis chuckled. “What does she eat for breakfast?”

“Cereal, toast, pancakes and waffles. Lunch is peanut butter or bologna sandwiches.” Grady waited for Alexis to finish her list.

Warming to the subject, he said, “It would probably also be nice if she was good at talking Savannah into doing things she doesn't particularly want to do—like homework or brushing her hair."

Alexis wrote down *diplomatic* and *persuasive* in big bold letters.

"And energetic," Grady added as an afterthought. "She needs to be able to keep up with Savannah, especially with the month-long summer break coming, since I don't plan to hire any more nannies."

Despite his decision to keep an emotional wall between them, Grady found himself fascinated by how quickly and delicately Alexis's hand moved as she took notes. "And last but not least, any woman who wants to come into our lives has got to be able to love my little girl as much as I do."

Alexis nodded in agreement. "Well, I can see I've got my work cut out for me."

Grady stood. "How soon can you introduce prospective mommies to Savannah?"

Alexis slipped her notebook in her briefcase. "I can have the first one here tomorrow, when Savannah comes home from school. But you're going to need to do something, too, Grady. You've got to fill out that questionnaire I gave you when we met at your office."

Grady scowled. "It has four hundred questions."

She held up a palm—her left hand, he couldn't help but notice. And the ring finger was bare.

"I know it's long," Alexis said. "I'm sorry about that. Just e-mail me the results when you're done. Our computer program will analyze the data and present us with a list of potential matches. We'll go from there."

GRADY SHOULD HAVE FELT good. The process of finding the replacement mother his little girl wanted had begun. Instead, he felt unsettled. Deeply, peculiarly so. Worse, every time he tried to figure out why that was, he ended up thinking about Alexis Graham instead.

He supposed that was because the straight-talking matchmaker was in charge of finding him a suitable wife, and her success rate of pairing up clients with someone to marry was close to one hundred percent.

Fortunately, a series of phone calls on his latest development project kept him busy the rest of the evening. The next morning was spent getting himself off to work and the unusually cooperative Savannah off to school.

As he arrived home with Savannah that evening, Alexis was pulling into his driveway.

He watched her get out of her white BMW.

Today, she was wearing a trendy teal suit that brought out the blue-green of her eyes. Her honey-colored locks had been drawn into a sophisticated french twist. A heart-shaped locket hung on a golden chain around her neck and nestled in the V of the silky teal blouse she wore beneath her jacket.

Her high heels clicked on the drive as she made her way toward his Cadillac Escalade.

Savannah, who had been pouting over the prospect of doing homework again, cheered up as she approached. "Daddy, it's my fairy godmother! She's here again!"

And she was supposed to have a likely candidate with her, Grady recalled.

He stepped down from the driver's seat and greeted her.

After returning the greeting, Alexis waved at Savannah, who was still strapped in her booster seat.

The little girl waved back vigorously.

"The first candidate should be here any second."

Grady breathed a sigh of relief. He really wanted to get this business over with as soon as possible. “Good,” he said.

As if on cue, a station wagon pulled into his wide circular drive in front of the house.

An attractive woman stepped out.

She had a kind face, short dark hair and brown eyes. She was wearing the type of clothes a well-to-do suburban mom might wear—tailored beige slacks, a matching summer-weight sweater set and sensible shoes.

Alexis made introductions. “Grady McCabe, I’d like you to meet Desdemona Bradford. Desdemona, this is Grady McCabe—the client I was telling you about.”

“Nice to meet you.” Desdemona shook hands with Grady, while Savannah, who had unsnapped her safety belt, looked on curiously before opening the rear passenger door.

Grady smiled and said hello, then turned to help his daughter from the car.

“Savannah, this is Ms. Bradford.”

“You can call me Desdemona,” she said with a smile.

“She’s a librarian and she knows a lot about storybooks,” Alexis stated.

“I brought some books for us to read.” Desdemona walked back to her station wagon to get them.

Savannah studied the librarian skeptically. She was more thrilled at the items accompanying the stack of brand-new books. “Cookies and milk!”

Desdemona shrugged. “I thought an icebreaker might be nice.”

“Good move,” Alexis murmured.

“You could join us,” Desdemona said to Grady.

He nixed the offer with a brief shake of his head. “Actually, I’ve got some phone calls to return. But thanks.”

Alexis, Desdemona and Savannah headed for the kitchen. Grady retired to the study that served as his at-home office.

An hour later, there was a knock at the door.

It was Alexis.

"How's it going?" he asked.

"I really like Desdemona. I think she's a wonderful person."

"But…?" Grady prompted.

"Maybe you should come out back and see for yourself," Alexis suggested.

Curious, Grady rose. He had taken off his suit jacket and tie, unfastened the top buttons on his shirt and rolled up the sleeves when he had sat down to work.

Alexis had also taken off her suit jacket—probably due to the unusually warm June afternoon. The sleeveless silk shell she wore moved fluidly about her slender torso, and exposed her arms to view. Grady had always considered himself a leg man—and Alexis's legs were spectacular—but for the first time he found himself equally entranced by the feminine shape of a woman's arms. There was no doubt about it—Alexis's shoulders, the supple curve of muscles in her upper arms, were every bit as alluring as the rest of her.

Not that he should be thinking this way.

Frowning, admonishing himself to stay on task, he followed her down the hall toward the back of the house. They walked through the breakfast room, out into the sunny family room and over to the French doors, which stood ajar.

Alexis put out a hand to stop him from stepping outside.

"Just stand here and observe a moment," she urged quietly.

"I want more cookies!" Savannah was saying.

"Sweetums, you've already had five."

"Daddy always lets me have six."

"No I don't," Grady murmured.

"Hush," Alexis said. She tapped the back of his hand lightly. "Pay attention!"

"All right. But you can't tell anyone I've given you another one!" Desdemona slipped another cookie from the bakery box balanced on top of the play fort platform.

"I want you to do somersaults for me," Savannah demanded.

Desdemona flushed and wrung her hands. "I can't. I'm too old, sweetums."

The girl sized her up shrewdly. "But that's what I want!" she demanded around a mouthful of cookie.

"How about we read books instead?" Desdemona pleaded.

Realizing she had the upper hand, Savannah shook her head. "No! I want you to do what I say...and I want you to do it now or I'm going to scream!"

"That's enough," Grady muttered.

He strode through the French doors and out onto the grass.

Desdemona had already slipped off her sensible shoes and was bending down, awkwardly attempting to figure out how to roll herself into a ball.

Grady stopped her with a hand on her shoulder, then removed the half-eaten cookie from his daughter's hand. "Savannah, you owe Ms. Bradford an apology."

"But, Daddy...!"

"Right now, Savannah."

The child flushed and sighed, then mumbled, "I'm sorry."

Grady picked up the library books and what was left of the box of cookies, then turned to Desdemona. "Let me walk you out," he said amicably.

"DADDY'S MAD AT ME," Savannah reported, when the two adults had disappeared through the wooden gate.

"With good reason, it would seem," Alexis answered. "You took advantage of Desdemona's kindness."

Savannah scuffed her sneaker in the grass and said in a low, hurt tone, "She didn't really want to play with me." She paused, to make sure Alexis was listening. "She just did it because she had to."

And Savannah, understandably, hadn't wanted any part of that. So she had acted out to get rid of her.

Without warning, Grady was back. "Don't you have homework to do, young lady?" he said.

Savannah's beleaguered look indicated she did.

"Is it in your backpack?" he continued.

She lifted one shoulder. "I guess so."

"What is it?"

"A picture. We're s'posed to finish coloring it."

Grady turned his daughter in the direction of the house. "All right. Please sit at the kitchen table and do your homework while I finish talking to Alexis."

Savannah tipped her head way back, so she could see her daddy's face. "*Then* can she stay for supper and play with me like she did last night?"

"I don't think so. Go. Now."

Savannah uttered a dramatic sigh and trudged toward the door. By the time she reached it, however, she was skipping. Whether in joy or relief, it was hard to tell.

Grady made sure she was out of earshot before he turned back to Alexis. "That was a disaster."

Alexis couldn't disagree. "It's not going to be easy to find a woman who will accept your criteria," she warned. "A marriage without sex or emotional intimacy is going to be a tough sell."

Grady ran a hand through his hair. "I'm sure there is someone," he stated in a low, aggravated tone.

Alexis contained her own frustration with effort. "I didn't say I was going to stop trying." She turned to face him. "I want Savannah to have a mommy as much as you and she do—I think she deserves that and so much more. But clearly the next candidate can't be someone who will let Savannah walk all over her."

Grady exhaled, his expression guilty. He massaged the muscles at the nape of his neck. "It's all those nannies I've had."

Alexis paused. "How many were there again?"

"At last count? Eight."

Wow. No wonder Savannah was having problems....

"The first two were great. They were a lot older—in their early sixties. They each stayed two years, before health woes forced them to retire." He sighed. "The next bunch were a lot younger. Physically able to keep up with Savannah, but each one wrong for some other reason."

"Such as...?"

"Where do I begin?" He took a deep breath before forging ahead. "Marabelle let Savannah get away with everything and anything, so she had to go. Liza tried to hit on me. Penny was always on the phone. Grendel had allergies that wouldn't let her spend any time outdoors. Xandra thought twelve hours of daily TV was just fine." He threw up his hands. "And last but not least, there was Maryellen, who, as it turned out, spent the majority of her time practicing her yoga on the living room floor while Savannah sat in a corner with a book."

It sounded like a nightmare. One that could have been avoided? "How'd you find so many bad child care workers?" Alexis asked curiously.

Grady stepped onto the shaded patio. "Don't ask me. They all had references. Experience." He waved her out of the sun, too. Once Alexis was beside him, he looked down at her and continued. "I guess the main problem was that the two older nannies I had were so great with Savannah, she was devastated when they left. Although both Olivia and Graciella keep in touch, it's not the same. To the younger, more energetic nannies, taking care of Savannah was just a job.

"By the time they came, she was old enough to observe the other kids in her preschool and kindergarten classes with their mothers, and realize what they had and she didn't. She wants a mother who loves her, and I don't blame her. I want that for her, too." Grady paused, his eyes clouding over. "I can't pretend I'm ever going to feel for another woman what I felt for my late wife. It's impossible."

Alexis nodded, understanding. "Grief like that can be very hard to overcome." But hopefully, not impossible, for him or for her. Otherwise, she'd never have what she wanted out of life, either.

An increasingly uncomfortable silence fell between them.

Finally, Grady looked deep into Alexis's eyes and stated quietly, "I still have to give my daughter what she needs. Even if it means entering into a marriage of convenience."

Alexis could see there was no changing his mind. A marriage of convenience it would be.

Chapter Three

"Burning the midnight oil?" Holly Anne looked pointedly at the extra-large latte in Alexis's hand, as she entered the conference room and took command.

Alexis smiled politely and made a mental note to work a little harder to cover up her growing disillusionment. As much as she was loath to admit it, the deep-seated frustration she felt this morning was only partly due to the heavy rainfall. It was more about the demanding client in her care.

The dozen other staffers already at the conference table regarded her with thinly disguised envy. Everyone there wanted the plum task of spending time with the delectably handsome, oh-so-eligible Grady McCabe. Of course, Alexis reassured herself practically, that probably would change if they knew how impossible he was going to be to match. It wasn't that she couldn't find a woman who would be willing to trade money for love. There was always someone viable in that category, of either sex. It was trying to find someone who would do so who would still be good for Savannah. That, Alexis wasn't sure was possible. And she did not want to let the adorable little girl down.

"Grady McCabe is particular," she said finally, wincing slightly when lightning lit up the dark morning sky.

Sandi Greevey sighed and said, over the rumble of thunder, "If you ask me, he's fooling himself if he thinks a woman is going to sign on without even the possibility of love or sex."

"I don't know," said another colleague, as rain lashed the windows with gusty force. "Hope burns eternal."

"Tell that to Russ and Carolyn Bass," Doreen Ross quipped.

Holly Anne frowned, clearly disappointed by the recent divorce filing that had flooded the morning airwaves. "I thought those two would last forever," she lamented.

So had Alexis, when she'd matched them.

"Just goes to show money doesn't buy happiness," Sally Romo said.

The receptionist walked in just then and handed Alexis a note.

She let out a breath slowly. Just what she needed to make her day even more difficult.

Six hours later, it was still raining heavily as she drove to Grady McCabe Enterprises's most recent acquisition.

The three-block area just south of downtown Fort Worth was blocked off as a construction zone and surrounded by a twelve foot high fence. Entrance to the muddy, rubble strewn demolition zone was monitored by an electric gate and a uniformed guard in a gray-and-black rain slicker.

"Alexis Graham, here to see Grady McCabe," she said when he stuck his head out the window of the gatehouse.

"He's expecting you, Ms. Graham. Proceed straight ahead to the last trailer. You can park behind it. Mr. McCabe is waiting inside."

Resentful that she was going to have to take her company-leased BMW through the car wash after this expedition, Alexis drove slowly through the gravel and mud, past a sign proclaiming this as the site of the new GME high-rise, to the quartet of construction trailers parked near the back of the sprawling lot.

There were six vehicles parked next to the last trailer.

She slid her BMW into the last available slot, grabbed her umbrella and briefcase, and got out.

THE MEETING HAD JUST broken up when the knock sounded on the trailer door.

Through the rain beating against the windows, Grady could see Alexis Graham standing on the wooden steps.

He rushed to open the door so she could get in out of the rain.

Water darkened the fabric of her vivid yellow trench coat. Her heels, stockings—even the hem of her raincoat—were coated with mud. Too late, he realized he should have suggested she dress more casually and maybe wear boots.

"Sorry I'm a little early," Alexis said, shaking out her umbrella. "I wasn't sure how long it would take to get here."

"No problem." Grady paused to introduce his four best friends: Dan, the architect of all his developments, and Travis, who owned the construction company that built them. Jack, the wiring genius whose company installed the networks, phones and satellite systems. And last but not least, Nate, the CEO of the Texas-based financial services company that was going to be leasing eighty percent of the available space in this latest project.

"Nice to meet you," Alexis said.

The four men murmured the same, grabbed their jackets and headed out.

Grady and Alexis were alone. Dumbstruck by how lovely she looked, with raindrops glistening on the tip of her nose and her cheeks, he said the first thing that came to mind. "Sorry about the weather...."

Merriment sparkled in her eyes. "You control that?"

Her teasing brought a smile to his face, too. "Sorry about having you meet me here in the middle of a monsoon," he corrected. "I thought the rain would have let up by now."

"We're in the midst of a tropical storm—or what's left of it this far inland. The precipitation isn't going away until tomorrow evening, at the earliest."

Normally, Grady would have known that. But he'd been too preoccupied lately. "Guess I should have paid more attention to the forecast."

"You seem to have your hands full."

Grady thought about Savannah's temper tantrum that very morning, when he'd told her she had to wear her school uniform—not her princess costume—to school, as always. "I do at that," he said dryly.

The phone rang, and Grady held up a hand, wordlessly asking her to wait before he pulled his BlackBerry from his pocket. He listened, but the words made no sense. He blinked in stunned amazement. "Could you repeat that…?"

Slowly but surely the meaning sunk in. Words not polite for fit company filled his head, the inner diatribe directed exclusively toward himself, for his increasingly poor parenting. "No. Thank you for letting me know. I'll be right there."

He ended the call with a push of a button.

Alexis looked at him and lifted a brow.

"It's Savannah," Grady said, already searching for his umbrella. "She's in trouble."

"WE CAN GO OVER your picks for the next introduction on the way over," he promised Alexis as the two of them headed back out into the rain.

She had insisted that this time he consider at least three

women, before selecting one. She hoped going through the process would show him what a valuable screening tool it was. Unfortunately, despite the fact she talked nonstop on the fifteen minute drive to Miss Chilton's Academy for Young Women, Alexis was fairly certain Grady didn't absorb a word of what she said.

Before she could quiz him on his thoughts, however, they were turning into the visitor parking lot of the city's oldest and most prestigious all-girl school. "Would you like me to wait in the car?" she said.

Grady shook his head. "It's too warm. I have no idea how long this will take. And I may need female reinforcement."

"Mind telling me what's going on, then?"

He held the umbrella over her head as they hurried toward the door. "The headmistress said something about a contretemps in ballet class, whatever that means. All I know is I am expected to come and get Savannah and take her home early—after stopping in the school office."

Grady held the door, then escorted Alexis through the lobby to the glass-walled principal's office. There, seated on a bench, was Savannah. Next to her was a little girl with long red hair and the kind of to-the-manor-born-air about her that Alexis had always hated.

Both were wearing hot-pink leotards, tights, tutus and ballet slippers. Their hair was askew. Their faces were flushed and pouty, but otherwise both looked fine.

The school secretary shot Grady a sympathetic look. "I'll let the headmistress, Principal Jordan, know that you are here."

Behind Grady, the door opened and closed.

An elegant red-haired woman in a slim black Prada skirt, electric-blue silk blouse and black Jimmy Choo boots glided in. She'd drawn a silk Hermes scarf over her head, to protect her hair. She whisked it down to lie against the diamond pendant around her neck. "Grady." She turned a regal nod in his direction.

"Hello, Kit," he replied. "Principal Jordan. I'd like you-all to meet Alexis Graham. She's a friend of the family."

Alexis tried not to read too much into the acknowledgment.

Savannah, however, was looking at her with an expression that clearly said, I'm so glad you're here! Now save me!

"Nice to meet all of you," Alexis said politely after the introductions had been made.

"What's going on?" Grady asked the principal.

"I'd like to know that myself," Kit Peterson said, clearly unhappy to be there under those circumstances.

"Savannah and Lisa Marie disrupted ballet class with a brawl. The teacher sent them to my office. Hair pulling, pushing, shoving, name calling—none of that will be tolerated at our school."

Grady looked at his daughter. Clearly in shock, he knelt down in front of her. "Honey, what do you have to say for yourself?"

Nothing, apparently, Alexis noted.

"She started it." Lisa Marie pointed the finger at Savannah, who remained stubbornly silent.

"I expect both girls to apologize to each other right now," Principal Jordan said.

"I'm sorry." Lisa Marie Peterson piped up immediately.

Her mom beamed in approval and relief, as did the headmistress.

Grady's little girl remained silent.

"Savannah?" he prompted.

Her expression grew stonier. She refused to look at her father, or any one else, even Alexis.

"Perhaps you should discuss this matter at home," Principal Jordan suggested, with slightly less patience.

Mrs. Hanford appeared with two backpacks and child-size rain slickers, one set of which bore outrageously expensive designer labels.

The principal looked at Grady, her frustration with his daughter apparent. "Although she does not have to do it right now if it is not sincere, I will caution you both that Savannah will not be allowed back in school until formal verbal restitution is made."

"I understand," Grady said.

So, apparently, did Savannah.

She wasn't budging.

"YOU OKAY WITH DROPPING by our house for a while, before we go back to the construction site to pick up your car?" Grady asked Alexis, after settling Savannah in the back seat and climbing behind the wheel.

"Sure."

"Good." His jaw set determinedly. "Because I still want to go over those files you brought, as soon as we get a minute."

"I wasn't certain you'd be interested…in, um…" Alexis paused to cast a brief glance at the back seat, where a glum Savannah was silently staring out of the rain-streaked window.

"In what?" Grady prompted, with a sidelong glance of his own—at her.

Alexis's cheeks warmed self-consciously beneath his scrutiny.

"Um..." She dropped her voice another notch. "Continuing your search for a new..." She gestured rather than complete the sentence out loud.

Grady exhaled, his own frustration with the situation apparent. "I think this latest 'contretemps' proves more than ever that I need to do something to provide the missing female guidance."

"There are other ways to do that." Alexis spoke before she could stop herself.

He gave her another, sharper look. "None I am interested in."

They both fell silent. Five minutes later, they turned into the driveway of his 1920s bungalow-style home in the River Crest Country Club area. The two-story gray stucco home with the dark gray roof and sparkling white trim was situated on a tree-lined cul-de-sac. Approximately half the size of many of the other luxurious homes in the area, it had an understated elegance and cozy, charming appeal, unobscured by the rain still pouring from the skies.

While Grady shut off the engine, got out of the Escalade and opened the rear passenger door, Alexis followed suit.

Grady lifted Savannah, who was clad in her yellow rain slicker and ballet slippers, down to the pavement. She didn't seem to care that her slippers were getting soaked for the second time. "Let me grab your backpack, then I'll carry you the rest of the way," he offered.

Finally, Savannah sparked back to life.

"No!" she shouted. Fists balled at her sides, she spun around, and before he could stop her, took off at a rapid pace for the front of the house. Several inches of water had gathered in the drive and water splashed up around her knees.

"Slow down!" Grady called, striding after her.

"No!" Savannah shouted again. Clearly in a temper, she

increased her speed, breaking into a run. And that was when it happened. The slippery soles of her flimsy slippers went out from beneath her and she went flying.

Alexis and Grady both gasped as Savannah landed facedown on the concrete drive, the bulk of the impact taken by her outstretched elbows and knees.

There was a moment's awful silence as her tiny body shook with soundless sobs, and then, a second later, loud wails.

Grady didn't hesitate. Tossing Savannah's backpack to Alexis, like a quarterback handing off a ball, he rushed forward and scooped his sobbing daughter into his arms.

He carried her through the rain to the front porch, punched in the code on the keypad next to the door, then stepped inside.

Alexis followed, her own eyes filling with moisture that had nothing to do with the rain coming down.

It didn't matter how old she was, or who was hurting. Alexis couldn't stand to see someone in pain. Never had been able to. Which was what had made the last years of her ill-fated marriage so very hard.

Grady continued through the foyer, down the hall and into the state-of-the-art kitchen, soothing his daughter with low, comforting words all the while.

Arms locked around his neck, Savannah cried uncontrollably.

He buried his face in her damp curls, gently patting her back, still soothing her verbally.

Finally, when she hiccupped and seemed to be calming down, he said, "Let me have a look at those 'owies'."

Savannah shook her head and clung all the more tightly.

Grady glanced at Alexis over the top of his daughter's head. "Can you…?"

"Sure." She slipped out of her drenched trench coat and moved closer, trying to inspect the damage. "Looks like she scraped both knees," she reported.

And that had to hurt!

"Check her elbows."

"We're going to have to get her slicker off."

"I'll help."

Still sobbing, Savannah refused to cooperate.

Together, the two adults finally managed, without Grady ever having to put his daughter down. "They look a little raw, but they're not..." *Bleeding,* Alexis mouthed. "Her palms, unfortunately, are both scraped raw."

Whoo boy, Grady mouthed back. "Savannah, honey, we need to get your owies cleaned up, and get you out of these wet clothes."

"No," Savannah wailed, even more hysterically. "It's going to hurt!"

"Then how about," Grady suggested, barely missing a beat, "we have your fairy godmother do it?"

ALEXIS HAD TO HAND IT to Grady—that was inspired. The suggestion got his daughter's tears stopped—momentarily at least—as she lifted her head and looked at Alexis. "Can you do it?" she whimpered. "Can you make it stop hurting?"

Alexis had made people in far worse straits comfortable. "Of course I can fix you up," she said calmly, slipping into caretaker mode. She tapped her index finger against her chin. "The question is," she added thoughtfully, "do you want to clean up those scrapes here in the kitchen, or in a nice warm bubble bath?" Which would do a better job and be a lot easier. "If we can get you in the tub to soak the dirt and germs out of your owies, I bet you can have a Popsicle, too."

Savannah sniffed and looked interested. "While I'm in the tub?" she asked incredulously.

Alexis turned to Grady, shifting the ball right back to him. "Daddy? Is it okay?"

Respected glimmered in Grady's eyes. "Sure."

"I'll tell you what. I'll get her in the tub, and you follow with Popsicles, the first aid kit and whatever dry clothes you want her to wear."

His lips curved into a grateful half smile. "No problem, fairy godmother."

Alexis looked back at Savannah, who was still ensconced in her daddy's strong arms. "Do you think you can walk upstairs, or do you want me to carry you?"

The child sniffed again. New tears trembled on her lashes. "I want you to carry me," she whimpered.

"I'll be happy to." Alexis held out her arms.

Savannah slid into them.

Together, they went up the stairs, down the hall, to the private bath in Savannah's suite. It was just as girlie and pink and suited for a princess as her bedroom was. "My goodness, you have a big selection of bubble baths!" Alexis exclaimed. She sat on the rim of the sunken tub, Savannah on her lap, and reached over to turn on the tap. "What kind do you want? Lavender? That's supposed to be very soothing. Or the one that smells like baby powder?"

"Baby powder." The lower lip was out as far as it would go.

Alexis snapped open the lid. "You want to help me pour it in?"

"Uh-huh." Savannah leaned over to let a generous amount stream beneath the tap. Bubbles sprung up immediately. She smiled slightly at the sight.

"I'm going to warn you," Alexis said. "It might sting when you first sit down in the tub, but then it's going to get much much better."

"I know," Savannah acknowledged miserably. "I've had to do this before when I falled down and hurted myself."

Alexis helped her slip out of her worse-for-wear ballerina outfit. "Me, too."

Savannah's eyes widened in amazement. "*You* fell down?"

"All the time when I was a kid," Alexis admitted with a rueful grin. "I had the worst time trying to learn to ride a bike…."

She was still regaling Savannah with stories of her own mishaps when Grady appeared, three pineapple-flavored Popsicles in hand.

Savannah brightened, seeing the frozen treats. Grady's eyes met Alexis's. "One for each of us." He telegraphed his gratitude, then turned back to his daughter. "So how are we doing?" he asked, lounging against the counter. "Are you okay?"

Savannah nodded and averted her eyes.

A sure sign, Alexis noted, that she was not.

"SAVANNAH ASLEEP ALREADY?" Alexis asked an hour later, when Grady joined her in the kitchen. She had been sitting at the table, catching up on her end-of-business-day e-mails, while he put his daughter to bed.

Grady nodded, his compassion for his little one evident in his gentle expression. "She didn't even get past the first page of the storybook."

Alexis sent him a commiserating glance and closed the lid of her laptop computer. She could finish that later. It was time to get back to setting up her primary client. "She had a rough day."

"I'll say." Appearing as restless and distracted as Alexis felt Grady plucked the skillet out of the dish drainer and put it away.

"But a good dinner," Alexis said, as he handled the very last of the cleanup. "Those two grilled cheese sandwiches and a glass of chocolate milk really did the trick," she teased.

Grady grinned, as if knowing it wasn't the healthiest array of foods he could have provided. He leaned against the sink, arms folded in front of him. "It was what she wanted," he said with an unapologetic lift of his broad shoulders. "Speaking of which..." He paused to look Alexis in the eye. "Thank you for staying and helping get her all fixed up. And hanging out with her while I made dinner. And eating with us once again."

He acted as if it had been a chore. It hadn't been. The truth was, Alexis hadn't felt so happy and content in a long time. Part of it was being around a child, because she loved kids. Had always wanted them. Fate had kept her from having any so far, but she hoped it wouldn't always be the case.

"It was my pleasure," she murmured, doing her best to keep the situation from getting too intimate.

"I'm serious." Grady strolled closer. "You were really good with her today."

Thinking maybe it was time they called it a night, Alexis pushed back her chair and stood.

The Savannah who'd hung out with them at suppertime was cuddly and cheerful and cooperative. Which made Alexis think all Grady's little girl really needed was a lot more tender loving care from people who genuinely cared about her.

Marriage, Alexis realized, might not be necessary.

Was it possible that a family friend—filling in as an occasional mom slash mother figure—would do?

Alexis wanted to suggest just that, rather than have Grady rush into a marriage that potentially might not work out over the long haul…and hence create a bigger void than Savannah already had in her life.

Unfortunately, Alexis's role as matchmaker, the responsibility for bringing in more business to a firm that had stood by her during the best and worst of times, precluded her doing so.

Aware that Grady was gazing at her quizzically, she turned the conversation back to the reason they were both here. "I enjoy spending time with her."

Grady studied Alexis. "She adores you, you know."

Alexis felt a lump of emotion well up in her throat, and the equally strong need to protest. "She barely knows me."

He stepped close enough to inundate her with his brisk, male scent. Some emotion she couldn't quite define flickered in his eyes. "She knows enough."

Alexis stared at him in confusion. She felt they were on the brink of some kind of epiphany. "Meaning…?"

"You're one of a kind, Alexis," Grady observed slowly. He cupped the side of her face with the palm of his hand.

Her breath hitched, even as she tilted her head up to his. This couldn't be happening. Could it? He couldn't be putting the moves on her. "What are you doing?" she murmured.

He gave her a look of determination that was as unexpected as it was compelling. His eyes shuttered to half-mast. "What I've wanted to do all day. Hell—" his head lowered and his mouth dropped even lower "—why not be honest here? From practically the first second we met…"

Alexis splayed both hands across his chest. His muscles were warm and hard beneath her palms, and she could feel his heart pounding. "That's…this…" Oh, hell, he was going to kiss her! "It's impossible…."

"No," he murmured. "It's not."

And then all was lost in the feel of his body pressed up against hers and the wonder of his lips moving over hers.

Chapter Four

The rational, practical part of Grady knew he shouldn't be kissing Alexis. Shouldn't be trying to ease the loneliness and isolation that had dominated his life for the last five years with the incredibly warm and tender woman in his arms. He should be walking away from the softness of her lips, and the femininity of her body pressed against his. Ignoring the sweet taste of her mouth, and the passionate way she kissed him back.

A physical relationship with her could only get in the way of what they were trying to do—find a mommy for Savannah… and a wife for him who would accept the limitations he set. A woman he could be honest with. A woman who understood. A woman Savannah could love, and who would love her in return.

Grady wanted a kind of wife Alexis didn't seem to think could be found. Unless… He broke off the kiss as the next idea hit.

Hands on her shoulders, he shifted her away. Working to keep himself from surrendering to temptation once again, he noticed the surprising vulnerability in her eyes. Her lip was trembling slightly, and she seemed as taken aback by the flare of desire between them as he was.

"Are you available?" Grady asked bluntly.

Alexis blinked and stepped away. "You mean single?"

For the first time in a long time, he felt fully, physically alive once again. With effort, Grady curtailed his spiraling emotions. "As a potential match."

"For you?" Alexis's brow lifted as the meaning of his words apparently sank in. She stepped back again and lifted both hands, as if to ward him off. "No. I'm not."

Grady hadn't gotten where he was in life by accepting no for an answer, especially when he wanted something as much as he suddenly wanted this. Eyes trained on hers, he asked, "Sure about that?"

Resentment laced her voice as she answered, "Matchmakers at my company are not allowed to date clients, Grady."

Most of the important decisions in his life were based on instinct. And right now it was telling him he'd already found the mother his daughter wanted and needed. A woman his daughter could love—and who would love Savannah back. "We're not talking about a date." Or anything near that insignificant. "We're talking about a match."

"Same thing," Alexis replied. "And it's out of the question, Grady."

Frustration tightened his muscles. "Why?"

She packed up her laptop, picked up her handbag and began searching for her cell phone. "Because you're in too much of a hurry to find someone and get this done." She pushed the words through gritted teeth.

He shrugged, not about to back down, now that he'd put the idea out there. "So I value efficiency."

She lifted her chin. "Efficiency is fine when it comes to business. But this isn't business, Grady, or at least it shouldn't be. It's your personal life."

He'd heard as much from the few friends and family who knew what he had planned. He shrugged. "So?"

She shook her head in mute exasperation. Finally looked him in the eye. "Ever heard the expression, 'Pick a spouse in haste and repent in leisure?'"

He exhaled. "More or less."

Alexis stepped closer, clearly not afraid to stand up to him. "When clients are in as much of a hurry as you are to get matched up," she explained, as if to someone in need of a great deal of counseling, "it's usually because they don't want to stop and think about what it is they are doing. Because—" she inched even closer "—they know if they do stop and think, they'll realize what a giant mistake they're making, and they won't go through with it."

Grady gazed down at her. "I won't back out," he stated confidently.

"You say that now. But when it comes time to commit to a lifetime without love, you may feel differently."

"I probably would if I thought I could love again," Grady said honestly. The sad thing was… "I don't."

"You really loved your wife that much?" Alexis whispered, backing away once more.

It was almost as if he could see an invisible force field go up around her heart. "Yes," he said.

A mixture of sadness and commiseration shone in Alexis's eyes. "And you still miss Tabitha."

Grady found himself wanting to talk about something he never discussed. "I don't know. Sometimes—" he shook his head, gulping around the sudden knot of emotion in his throat "—I can barely remember her. Other times, the void in my life…" He paused, searching for words. "Let's just say I really feel it."

More gently now, Alexis asked, "How did you meet?"

Grady lounged against the kitchen counter again. He took a deep breath, let it out. "Tabitha was an interior designer who specialized in commercial buildings. I was right out of college and had just purchased my first run-down commercial space. The location was good. The interior of the building was not. I wanted to redo it and then lease it out." He smiled reminiscently. "She helped me achieve my dream. After that, we were inseparable. Worked on one project after another and got married three years after we met."

Alexis went back to the table and took a notepad and pen out of her briefcase. She sat down in the chair and began to write. "Was she close to your family?"

Grady watched Alexis's movements, for the first time realizing she was left-handed. "Yes."

She looked up, intent. "Is that important to you—that the person you marry be loved by your family?"

He nodded.

"What about prenups?" The questions now were rapid-fire. "Are you going to ask for one?"

"I didn't before," he admitted, remembering he'd been called a fool for that, too, by everyone who knew his own earning potential, plus what he one day stood to inherit from the trust his folks had set up for him.

Aware that she was still waiting for an explanation, Grady said, "When I married it was for life. I just didn't know Tabitha's would be so short."

Empathy radiated in Alexis's eyes.

She took a moment to consider that, then asked, "When you marry again, will it be for life?"

Grady hoped so. But he knew, under these circumstances, which were quite different, he had to take steps to protect himself and Savannah from anyone who might be in it purely for the money. He regarded Alexis steadily. "This time, I will require prenups for both of us, should the union not work out. Although I would hope and expect it would never come to divorce."

Alexis made a face and kept writing. "If you ever get married again," she murmured, in a cynical tone he hadn't heard her use before. She paused, looked up. "I'm not convinced you will. Not without being in love."

Grady stayed rooted in place. Not sure why, only knowing he was enjoying the sparks of mutual aggravation arcing between them as much as he had enjoyed kissing her a few minutes before. She seemed to be reluctantly attuned to their chemistry, too. "If you expect me to back out," he countered, "then you don't know me very well."

Alexis nodded. "Exactly."

A fact, Grady thought, that could easily be remedied. "So back to you and me..."

She drew a deep breath that lifted her breasts. "There is no you and me."

Grady noted she wasn't looking at him—a sure sign there could be a "them", given half a chance. He pushed away from the counter, closed the distance between them, took her wrist and raised her to her feet. "That kiss we shared just now said otherwise."

Twin spots of color touched her cheeks. "That kiss meant nothing," she declared. But her breathing was slightly agitated.

"On the contrary." He made note of the absence of her customary cool as he tucked a hand beneath her chin. "It was a wake-up call to me."

She jerked back abruptly. "And what did it say?"

Grady lifted both his hands and determinedly held his ground. "That maybe, just maybe, I've been selling myself short with the parameters I set for my next spouse."

ALEXIS HAD THOUGHT, after the kiss—and Grady's equally inane suggestion that they consider marrying for his daughter's sake—that he couldn't surprise her further. She was wrong. Momentarily tabling her decision to call a cab to take her back to her BMW, which was still parked at his construction site, she sat back down for the third time in twenty minutes and picked up her pen, determined to get as much information as possible from him while he was in the mood to talk. "Okay, obviously you've refined your notion of what you want in a potential relationship. What are you looking for now?"

"Someone who could enjoy sex without the romance and a child…and a life together as man and wife."

She tried not to leap to the conclusion that the kiss they had shared had in any way jump-started Grady's latent physical needs. "But no love," she ascertained, a great deal more coolly than she felt.

"I've already had the love of a lifetime. To think lightning would strike twice…" He paused, his guard going up again. "Let's just say the odds are very much against it."

Grady took a seat at the table catty-corner from her, and surveyed her with surprising intimacy. "Oddly enough, you look as if you understand why I can't love anyone else the way I loved my wife."

Maybe this was an area where they could in fact relate. Finding she wanted him to know at least a bit about her, she said quietly, "I do. I was married, too."

He was silent, absorbing that, then dropped his gaze to the unadorned ring finger on her left hand. "And?"

It was her turn to talk about matters she found difficult to discuss. "I got married right after college, too. We were together for seven years. If Scott hadn't died, two years ago, we would still be together now."

The loss she felt was reflected in Grady's eyes. "What happened?"

Alexis swallowed. Her voice took on a raspy note. "Cancer. He'd had it as a kid. Had been in the clear for almost fifteen years. And then the leukemia came back and..." Their lives, their dreams, everything they had hoped for and wanted had been turned upside down. Alexis shook her head. Even now, it seemed like such an impossible, bad dream. She forced herself to go on, "For two years, he had all the latest treatments. Something would start to work, we'd think we were out of the woods, and then...we weren't. He got sicker and sicker, until finally nothing worked and he just couldn't fight it anymore."

Grady reached across the table and took her hand. The feel of his strong fingers around hers was as warm and reassuring as his presence. "I'm so sorry, Alexis."

She hadn't felt the need to lean on a man for a long time. She felt it now. Finding comfort in the empathy in his eyes, even as tears blurred her vision, she said, "So am I. I still love Scott. I always will. But I also know that part of my life is over."

Grady withdrew his hand reluctantly. Sat back. "So you will marry again."

Alexis nodded, knowing what she had just recently begun to realize herself—that the only way to leave sorrow behind was to move on. Not just partially, but all the way. "If I find love again, you bet I will." Because marriage was the best thing that had ever happened to her.

"What if you don't find true love again—at least not on that heart and soul level?" he asked, practical as ever.

She knew where this conversation was going. She cut him off at the pass. "I'm not going to settle, Grady. I'm not going to do what you're contemplating, and enter into a marriage of convenience. I'd rather be alone than be with someone and *feel* alone."

Deciding this session had gotten way too intimate for either of their sakes, she stood, began to pack up her belongings one last time. "In the meantime, I need you to look through the potential matches I've selected for you. If any of those three women appeal to you, or seem—on paper and on videotape—as if they might be a good match, let me know and I'll set something else up as quickly as possible."

"Under the guise of this match being a friend of yours, instead of a potential mommy," Grady cautioned.

Normally, there was no way Alexis would agree to anything so convoluted. But then, a little girl's feelings were not usually involved. She nodded. "Savannah may figure it out, if we have to do this too many times. But I'm willing to go with that plan as long as it works."

THE NEXT MORNING, Alexis's cell phone rang just as she was heading out the door. Caller ID indicated it was Grady. Wondering if he had found a match who intrigued him, she picked up. "Hello, Grady."

"Good morning, Alexis."

It was ridiculous, really, how happy she was to hear his low, gravelly voice. Ridiculous how warm it suddenly felt in the small studio apartment she had lived in since her late husband had first gotten sick.

Frowning, Alexis walked over to the window unit in charge of cooling the place, and turned the dial to maximum. Enjoying the resulting blast of icy air, she sat down on the windowsill in front of the air conditioner. "What can I do for you this morning?" she asked.

"How much do you know about defiant little girls?"

Not the response she was expecting. Alexis promptly switched into problem solving mode. "Enough, I think. Why?" She tensed in concern. "What's going on?"

Grady exhaled. "It's Savannah. She's refusing to go to school. She won't tell me why."

Alexis unbuttoned her jacket. Was it her imagination or was the air blowing out behind her warming slightly once again? She turned around and fiddled with the dial. "Is it because of what happened with Lisa Marie Peterson yesterday?"

"I don't know. She won't talk to me."

Alexis heard the mixture of hurt and frustration in his voice. "I'm not sure what to do." He sighed. "I think she needs a woman's tender loving care—if that makes any sense."

It made perfect sense to Alexis. Women were better at handling certain things, men others. "Where are you?" Deciding to give her air conditioner—which had been working overtime lately—something of a rest, she switched the dial back to low.

"Home."

Alexis retrieved her briefcase and purse. "I'll be right over and see what I can do."

"Thanks." Grady's relief was palpable. "You're a lifesaver."

Maybe not that, Alexis thought as she let herself out of her studio apartment and walked outside to her car. But she figured she could be of some help.

Grady was waiting for her when she arrived at his home fifteen minutes later. He was dressed for work, in a suit and tie. Savannah was still in the pink princess pajamas she had put on after her bath the night before. She was seated at the kitchen table, her breakfast of cold cereal and glass of juice in front of her, untouched. She had her right arm stretched out on the table, her head on top of that, face hidden from view.

Grady looked at Alexis, clearly concerned. Now that she was here and could see what he was dealing with, Alexis was concerned, too. She set her purse on the kitchen counter and walked over to the table. "Bad morning?" she asked gently.

Savannah looked up at Alexis, her blue eyes swimming with tears. She nodded, let out a heartfelt sob, and thrust herself into Alexis's waiting arms.

IF GRADY HAD HAD ANY doubts before, he had none now as he watched Alexis gather Savannah in her arms and sit down, cradling her in her lap. Alexis had a mother's loving touch.

And Savannah knew it.

"Oh, honey," Alexis soothed, stroking one hand through his little girl's tangled ringlets, another down her back. "It's all right."

Stubbornly, Savannah shook her head. "No, it's not," she insisted.

Now that, Grady thought, sounded like his headstrong daughter.

Savannah sniffed. Ignoring him completely, she drew back to look into Alexis's face.

"Are you still upset about the fight you had yesterday with Lisa Marie?" Alexis pressed.

Grady had asked the same question—to no avail—so he was surprised to hear his daughter answer right away.

"I don't want to say sorry to her!"

Was that what this was about? Grady wondered.

"Because…?" Alexis prodded.

Savannah's whole body tensed. "She's mean!"

"Mean how?" Grady asked. He pulled a chair up next to them and sat down.

Savannah cuddled closer to Alexis, but told him, "She makes fun of me and I don't like it!"

"Be that as it may, that's no reason to get in a hair-pulling fight with her," he stated firmly.

Over Savannah's head, Alexis gave Grady a look that told him very clearly to back off and let her handle this.

"I'm not going to say I'm sorry," Savannah repeated, even more stubbornly.

Exasperated, Grady pointed out, "Then you are not going to be able to go back to school." To his chagrin, his daughter clearly didn't care.

"Hmm. Well…" Alexis grew thoughtful. "I suppose that is one option."

Savannah looked up in surprise.

Grady gazed at her in shock.

"You could stay home alone, away from all your friends, and never get to play on the school playground again. You'd probably be a little lonely, and maybe bored. But I guess it would be okay."

Grady gave Alexis a look Savannah couldn't see. This was not helping! Alexis ignored him.

"But..." Savannah's resolve began to waver, just a bit.

Alexis shrugged. "Or you could apologize and say you were sorry you lost your temper, because I'm sure that is true. I'm sure you were not happy that you let someone push you into behaving that way. Because that's not who you are, Savannah McCabe." She looked meaningfully at Grady's daughter. "You're not the playground bully who shoves everyone else around and makes them feel bad. You're the girl who is nice to everybody, the girl who just wants to be friends."

For once, Savannah didn't disagree.

"What did she say to you, anyway, to get you so mad?" Grady asked gently after a moment.

Savannah's lower lip shot back out. "Lisa Marie said I did not have a fairy godmother and that I was never going to have a mommy, 'cause my mommy was dead."

Whoa, Grady thought. That *was* cruel.

Alexis looked as upset as he felt. "That wasn't very nice, was it?" she said quietly.

"No." Savannah looked relieved to have emotional backup.

"And it's not true. Because—" Alexis smiled "—as we've already established, I am going to help your daddy find a new mommy for you. Now, it's not going to be easy, because sometimes these things take awhile. But if you are persistent, you can make your dreams come true. The question is, how do we handle this?" Alexis asked as Savannah's brow furrowed. "Do you want me to talk to Lisa Marie and tell her I am indeed your fairy godmother, so to speak?"

"You'd really do that?" Grady found himself cutting in once again.

Alexis grinned, the picture of maternal confidence. "I'll

even go with you and Savannah when she apologizes to Lisa Marie and anyone else who feels the need for an apology."

Savannah sat there on Alexis's lap, clearly considering.

"Of course, we can do this whenever you want, Savannah," Alexis continued amiably, "but I have always found that when you don't particularly *want* to do something, it's better to just do it and get it over with."

"ALEXIS GRAHAM, you are a miracle worker," Grady declared an hour later, as the two of them walked out of Miss Chilton's Academy for Young Women.

She waved away his praise. "Savannah just needed moral support." And as Grady had already intuited, a mother figure's loving presence in her life, to help her with some of her girl problems.

Grady paused next to Alexis's BMW. "Do you think Lisa Marie will leave her alone now?"

Alexis hit the unlock button on the keypad and opened the door to let the searing summer heat out of the vehicle. "Knowing female bullies—probably not." She tossed her purse onto the passenger seat, next to her briefcase, and turned back to Grady. Trying not to notice how his dark hair shone in the morning sunlight, she predicted, "It'll just be more of a stealth operation than ever."

With the mean-girls-in-training in Savannah's kindergarten class doing everything they could under the school administration's radar to taunt the little girls they perceived as undeserving of kindness and respect.

Grady leaned against his Escalade, which was parked next to her sedan. He pushed the edges of his suit coat back and braced his hands on his waist. "So what do we do?"

Alexis gestured vaguely, wishing like heck she could do

more to protect his little girl from even the potential of hurt. "You do what all parents do. Keep an eye out for trouble. Help Savannah learn to develop a thicker skin and rise above the petty manipulations, of which, sad to say, there will be plenty in the years ahead."

"You sound so cynical."

Maybe because, Alexis thought, in this one aspect, she was. "Your wife never had problems with female bullies?"

"I don't know. It's not something we talked about. Did you?"

"As a child, yes." These days, she could take care of herself in the mean girl department.

Grady favored her with an appreciative smile. "That's no surprise, I guess. It's usually the good-looking girls who get chased the most on the playground."

If the two of them had been children, Alexis figured Grady would be chasing her right now.

"And that makes the other girls jealous," he continued.

And sometimes ridiculing and vindictive. Finding herself in no more of a hurry to get to the office than Grady appeared to be, Alexis fiddled with the car keys in her hand. "Which is why, I guess, you put Savannah in an all-girls school, to keep her away from little boys?"

Grady shook his head. He took off his suit coat, opened the back door of his car and tossed it in. "She's going there because that's where Tabitha attended school, and I promised her before Savannah was born that any daughters of ours would go there, too."

So, it was a sentimental choice. That made more sense. Alexis nodded thoughtfully. "About those three profiles that I gave you last night..."

"I looked through them," he reported. "Twice, as a matter of fact. I couldn't really see any of them being a good match."

Alexis sighed.

"I might feel differently, meeting them in person, if there was some spark between them and Savannah, but..."

Alexis wasn't sure whether she was relieved he hadn't been drawn to anyone else, or frustrated to the point she wanted to shout aloud in irritation. She had been so sure those three women were all his type. "I'll keep looking," she promised.

"HOW COME WE'RE going shopping before I do my homework, Daddy?" Savannah asked.

Because Alexis had called with a potential match she was very excited about, and wanted them both to meet. Having decided, however, that it probably wasn't a good idea to have Savannah giving any future mothers the runaround before they even saw if there was any chemistry there, Alexis and Grady were taking a new approach. They were doing this one on the down-low.

Did he feel good about it? No. Did he think the end justified the means? Yes.

If Savannah's meltdown yesterday afternoon and again this morning had shown him anything, it was that his little girl needed a woman's presence in her life. And since Alexis had made it clear she wasn't interested in being anything more than a temporary stand-in, he had no choice but to keep looking.

"We're going to the mall because it's raining again, and you can't play outside today," Grady said. Another storm had blown in that afternoon, which wasn't that uncommon for June. "Plus I figured, since you did a very grown-up thing this morning and apologized nicely to everyone, even though you still don't think you did anything wrong—"

"That's 'cause I didn't, Daddy," Savannah interrupted.

Figuring they'd leave the discussion about solving conflict in a peaceful manner for another day, Grady continued "—that we would take advantage of the fact that there is a covered parking deck as well as a very good ice cream shop in this mall, and take some time to smell the roses."

"There are flowers there, too?"

Grady shook his head. "It's an expression."

"Huh?" Savannah blinked.

"I meant we should enjoy ourselves today," he clarified.

Savannah skipped along, holding his hand. He grinned down at her. This had been a good idea. One that might make the inevitable take-home work sheet a little easier to get completed before dinner this evening....

"Hey, Daddy, look!" Savannah got so excited she jumped up and down.

There, on the other side of the mall atrium, were two blondes standing side by side in front of a shoe store.

"It's Alexis! And some lady!" Savannah jumped again and clapped her hands together. "Can we say hi to them, Daddy? Please! Please! Please! Please!"

"Calm down, honey, and yes we can." Before he could say anything else, Savannah raced off across the floor. She skidded to a halt just short of Alexis, and taking a deep breath, looked up at her shyly.

Alexis turned away from the display of shoes she and her companion had been admiring. She dropped the shopping bag she was carrying and knelt down, arms open wide. The way, Grady figured, a mother would greet her child. "Well, hello there, sweetheart," she said. "Fancy meeting you here!"

Savannah barreled into Alexis's embrace. Small arms wreathed around her neck and she held on tight for a long time. One would have thought, by his little girl's reaction, she hadn't seen Alexis in ages, instead of just seven hours ago….

"What are you doing here?" Alexis asked at last, when they had stopped hugging each other and were face-to-face again.

"Daddy and I are having ice cream! Want some?"

Alexis looked up at Grady.

A glimmer of apology shone in her eyes. This wasn't going exactly the way she had hoped, but it was pretty much how Grady would like to see things evolve.

"We'd love to have you join us," he said cordially. He looked over at the pretty blonde next to Alexis. She was thirty something, with a trim, athletic figure, kind eyes and what appeared to be an abundance of energy. He held out his hand. "I'm Grady McCabe. My daughter, Savannah."

"Nice to meet you. I'm Tina Weinart."

"Tina's a nurse at the Children's Hospital," Alexis said, getting slowly and gracefully back to her feet.

"We'd love to have you join us, too, if you can," Grady told Tina.

"I'd love to." She smiled, then looked at Savannah. "I heard you had a fall yesterday."

The little girl slipped her hand in Alexis's and pressed in close as they walked to the ice cream store at the end of the aisle. She demonstrated by holding up first one knee, then the other. Beneath the tartan skirt of her school uniform, two Band-Aids were visible on each knee. Savannah then held up the heels of her hands. No Band-Aids there; the scrapes had been light enough to do without. "It hurt!" she declared. They entered the shop and took a horseshoe-shaped booth in the center. Savannah slid across the banquette seat and onto Alexis's lap. She rested her head on Alexis's chest and continued recounting her sad tale to

Tina. "And that's how come I'm not supposed to run in the rain. 'Cause," she added for emphasis, "I might fall down."

Tina nodded, clearly as enthralled with Grady's little girl as he was.

Savannah, however, had affection only for Alexis. Forty-five minutes later, when they'd finished their sundaes, Alexis took her into the ladies' room to wash her hands and face.

Tina looked at Grady. "She's adorable. I'd like to get to know her better—without Alexis around. Otherwise, I'm not sure she'll even give me a chance to connect with her."

Grady knew Tina had a point. Alexis was a hard act to follow. Especially where his daughter was concerned.

"SO? WHAT'D YOU THINK of Tina?" Alexis asked Grady over the phone later that evening, after Savannah was fast asleep.

He tried not to think how lonely it was, with Alexis at her place and he at his, or how much he and Savannah had both missed having her there with them during the evening routine.

"Tina was very nice. Personable," Grady responded. "I'm a little concerned about the lack of chemistry between her and Savannah, though." The affection and interest, while genuine, had seemed all on Tina's side.

"Tina mentioned she wanted to get together with the two of you, without me," Alexis continued, with a cheerfulness that sounded slightly forced. "I think it's a good idea. In this case, four probably is a crowd."

Grady agreed with that. He just wasn't sure they were talking about the same three. Still, he knew Savannah needed a mommy, and Tina was happily volunteering to enlist…on his terms.

Alexis was not….

"I haven't told Savannah yet, but Tina's going to be stopping by tomorrow evening with a new puzzle she thought Savannah would enjoy. I'll step out to make a phone call—and we'll go from there."

There was a slight pause. "You'll let me know how it goes?" Alexis's voice was brisk.

Grady reminded himself he was done wishing for the impossible, and adapted Alexis's businesslike attitude. "You'll get a call as soon as the 'next date' concludes," he said.

Chapter Five

Grady's visit from Tina was slated for five o'clock Friday evening. At four forty-five, Alexis received a call from him. "I've got a problem," he said without preamble.

Instinctively, she quipped back, "You seem to have a lot of those lately."

He sighed. "No joke, Sherlock." The ding of a car door opening sounded in the foreground. "I don't have much time to talk. I'm on my way into the school to pick up Savannah from her after-school program."

Alexis hoped he hadn't changed his mind about Tina. On an intellectual level, anyway, she knew the two might be a good match. Certainly, Tina would be a good mother to Savannah.... Emotionally, well, Alexis couldn't help but feel a little wistful that she and Grady were not looking for the same things in their future.

"What can I do for you?" she said more seriously, pushing away the memory of their one fantastic kiss.

"Run interference," Grady stated.

Alexis furrowed her brow in confusion. "How?"

"Get ahold of Tina. Make some excuse. Tell her this evening is not a good time."

Alexis pushed the send button on the e-mail she had just written to another client, and rocked back in her desk chair. “May I ask why?”

When he answered, his tone was wry. “I just had a call from my parents. Surprise! They’re in town for the weekend and they want to stay with us.”

Alexis had lost her own parents two years after she got married, so she no longer had to deal with what they would think about what she said and did. But she could still imagine all too well their reactions to things.

“I can see where that would be complicated.”

“You have no idea. Anyway, would you please call Tina and tell her we’ll have to reschedule for next week? I’ve been trying to reach her on her cell, and all I get is voice mail. And I can’t keep trying, because of course I don’t want Savannah to know….”

Alexis reached for Tina’s contact numbers. “What if I can’t find her?”

Grady groaned. “Let’s hope you can, because by the time I get to my place with Savannah, my parents will be there, too.”

Alexis tried all the numbers she had for Tina—to no avail. Working quickly, she shut down her office computer, grabbed her briefcase, purse and keys, and headed for Grady’s home.

By the time she got there, it was too late.

There were three cars in the drive. Grady’s Escalade, a bright yellow pickup truck with WILDCAT on the license plate and a Wyatt Drilling Company logo on the side and a Toyota with a Children’s Hospital Staff parking sticker.

Still trying to figure out how she was going to usher a disappointed Tina out of the house, Alexis walked up to the door and rang the bell. Grady opened it. The look on his face said *Rescue Me.*

"It's Alexis!" Savannah broke away from her grandparents and ran toward her. The little girl had on the athletic clothing she had worn for the after-school soccer practice, and her curls were more a mess than ever. She threw her arms around Alexis's waist, then turned to her grandparents and said, "This is my fairy godmother!"

GRADY WASN'T SURE what was worse—the coming together of all these people at exactly the wrong time, or the look on everyone's faces. His parents were clearly amused—and perplexed—while Savannah was deliriously happy. Tina Weinart looked ticked off. He was doing his best to keep a poker face. Only Alexis looked pleasantly composed—but then she was clearly in her element. "Hello, everyone," she said with a smile.

"Are you going to play with me today and have dinner with us again?" Savannah asked.

"Actually, I came over to see if Grady's company was still interested in tickets for the cancer research fund-raiser tomorrow evening," Alexis said. She looked around the room. "I'm on the committee that's hosting it."

Good save, Grady thought. "Absolutely. If a table is still available."

"I'm sure we can fit one in."

"Great. Let me get my checkbook."

"Can I go?" Savannah asked, when he had walked back out into the foyer.

Grady shook his head. "It's just for grown-ups, honey."

Her face fell.

"Children's Hospital has fund-raisers you can attend," Tina Weinart interjected.

Savannah brightened. "Really?"

She nodded. "I think the next one is in July. But in the meantime, I can arrange a private tour of the hospital, if you like."

The little girl looked interested.

Grady opened his checkbook and glanced at Alexis. "If you'll tell me who to make it out to..."

"I'd like to go, too," Tina said, opening her purse.

"We'll babysit," Grady's mother offered. She extended her hand to Alexis. "By the way, I'm Josie Wyatt McCabe, Grady's mother. This handsome guy next to me is my better half and Grady's father, Wade McCabe."

Her husband chuckled.

Alexis smiled. "I'm Alexis Graham."

"Do you know Tina?" his mother continued, obviously curious as to why he had two beautiful single women in his house at one time. Up to now, he had hardly been socializing, never mind actually dating.

Before Grady could formulate a reply, Tina jumped in to explain, "Alexis is the matchmaker who introduced Grady and me to each other."

EVERYONE WAS SO STUNNED, the foyer so quiet, you could have heard a pin drop, Alexis noted. Fortunately, the implications of what Tina had just said had gone completely over Savannah's head. The child frowned. "What's a matchmaker?"

Wade McCabe, a handsome man with silver threading his short dark hair, explained kindly, "That's a person who helps like-minded people get to know each other."

Again, the explanation was too adult—and circumspect—for Savannah to completely understand. Which was, Alexis figured, the intent.

Josie propped her hands on her blue-jeans-clad hips. Tall

and slender, with glossy brown hair, the youthful-looking woman fixed her azure eyes on her son, as if indicating they would talk—when the time was right.

Alexis smiled cordially. "Tina, I have something I'd like to discuss with you, so if you'll—"

Her client dug in her heels. "Actually, Alexis, it's not a good time for me. I haven't given Savannah her new puzzle yet."

"It'll just take a moment," Alexis insisted.

Savannah ambled back to Tina's side. She peered in the cloth carryall. "Can I see?"

"Certainly." Tina smiled, digging into it. "If it's all right with your daddy, of course."

Apparently realizing the benefit of having Savannah out of earshot, at least momentarily, Grady nodded and said, "Of course. Honey, why don't you take Tina outside? You can sit on the patio and look at the puzzle, and I'll bring out some lemonade for everyone in a minute. I want to talk to Grandma and Grandpa first."

"Okay, Daddy. Alexis, do you want to come, too?" Savannah asked.

"Alexis needs to stay here," Grady replied. "But we'll all be out in a moment."

Tina and Savannah departed.

When the back door had opened and shut, Grady gestured toward the formal living room. "Why don't we sit down?"

His parents sat on the sofa. Following reluctantly, Alexis perched on the edge of a wing chair. Grady took the other.

"We know how tough Tabitha's death was for you, and we're happy you're ready to move on, at long last," his mother began. "But—sorry, Alexis—a *dating service?*"

"Since when have McCabe men had any trouble finding a woman to go out with?" his dad asked.

"Not to mention the improbability of finding someone via third party," his mother continued.

"Isn't that what a blind date is?" Grady continued amiably.

His father chuckled. "Got a point there, son." He looked at Alexis. "How do you match people up?"

"We have detailed questionnaires about hobbies, interests and opinions, and we run a computer program that sorts out likely matches. But that's just the first step. After that the program sorts information gathered in one-on-one interviews with clients. When all the appropriate data is collected, we present the client with promising candidates. They review files and look at video interviews of likely matches, and if a rapport seems possible, we set up a meeting. If that doesn't work out, we set up another, and so on until a match is made."

"How long does it usually take?" Wade asked.

She shrugged. "Anywhere from weeks to months or even a year or two. We keep looking as long as the client is interested."

"ForeverLove.com is the agency the Basses' daughter, Carolyn, used," Grady added.

It was all Alexis could do not to wince.

"Russ and Carolyn Bass are getting divorced," Josie said. "I talked to her mother a couple of weeks ago. She said that, in retrospect, Carolyn is sorry she ever went that route."

Alexis imagined she was.

"Did you know them?" Josie asked.

Reluctantly, Alexis admitted, "I matched them."

FOR THE SECOND TIME that afternoon, silence fell. Alexis stood. "I think I'll check on Tina, see if she's ready to go."

Grady stood, too. "I'll walk with you."

He fell into step beside her. As they reached the hall, he

took her lightly by the arm. "But first, I do want to give you a check for the benefit tomorrow evening, before it slips my mind. If you'll come in here..." Cupping her elbow, he steered her into his study and shut the door behind them.

Alexis felt the warmth in her cheeks. She told herself it was because she was embarrassed she'd put him on the spot that way, pretending she was there for charity. "You don't have to purchase any tickets. Never mind an entire table—"

Grady took the checkbook and pen out of his shirt pocket. "It's for a good cause. I want to support it. I'm sure I can round up however many people need to be there, as my guests. Perhaps they'll write checks, too."

Alexis couldn't say no to the help it would provide in finding a cure. "Thank you," she said, gratefully.

Grady sat on the edge of his desk and opened the checkbook on his thigh. "How many at each table?"

Alexis looked down at the rock solid muscles beneath his suit pants, and tried not to think how those same muscles had felt pressed up against hers. "Eight. At a cost of two hundred fifty dollars per person."

He wrote a check for two thousand dollars and gave it to her. Their hands touched as they made the exchange. "I'm sorry if my parents embarrassed you."

Aware of how her fingers were still tingling, she slid the check into her purse. "It's no problem," she managed to reply.

"It is for me." He caught her by the shoulders before she could step away. "I believe in what you're doing for me and for Savannah."

Alexis only wished she could say the same.

She thanked him and they walked together toward the back of the house.

A few moments later, they stepped out onto the patio.

Savannah was cuddled up next to Tina, as they put in the last two puzzle pieces. "There you are," Tina said to Grady with a smile.

"Daddy, this puzzle is awesome!" Savannah said, showing him the finished picture of brightly colored fish.

Grady admired her accomplishment with obvious paternal pride. "Did you thank Tina?" he asked.

"She did," the nurse told him with a smile.

"Tina, could I speak to you privately?" Grady glanced at Alexis. "If you could just hang out here for a second..."

Alexis had the feeling Tina would refuse to go, if she thought she was leaving a rival for Savannah's affection behind. "Actually, I need to get going." She bent down to the little girl. "I just wanted to say goodbye before I left."

"Will you come and see me again?" Savannah asked.

Alexis smiled, not sure what to say. Was her presence helping or hurting here? If it interfered with Savannah's ability to bond with a woman who wanted to become her mommy—and Grady's wife—her growing relationship with Savannah could hardly be considered a positive thing.

"Alexis will definitely be back," Grady reassured her.

Knowing Grady still wanted to talk to Tina alone, Alexis held out a hand to his daughter. "Want to come with me while I say goodbye to your grandparents?"

Savannah slipped out of the curve of Tina's arm. "I had fun doing puzzles with you," she told the other woman shyly.

"I had fun spending time with you, too," Tina answered fondly.

Hand in hand, Alexis and Savannah set off.

THREE HOURS LATER, Holly Anne stopped by Alexis's office. "What has you here so late on a Friday evening?"

Not much, Alexis thought. *Jealousy. Guilt. Worry.* She fretted that she wasn't doing the right thing for Savannah, in fixing her dad up with someone he swore he would never be able to love. She sighed heavily. She'd never admit this to her boss, but she was also starting to wonder if her budding feelings for Grady—complex and mixed up as they were—had begun to cloud her judgment.

"Grady McCabe?" Holly Anne guessed, coming all the way into the office.

She nodded. These days it was always Grady McCabe. "I'm just pulling up some more profiles for him to peruse." Alexis studied the photo on the screen, ignoring her own lingering resistance to this matchmaking assignment, then hit the print command once again.

Her boss moved to the window and looked out at the dusk falling softly over downtown Fort Worth. "Tina Weinart didn't work out?"

All business, Alexis rose, plucked the pages out of the printer and added them to the folder on her desk. "She did better with Savannah the second time they met, but I just can't see her with Grady McCabe."

Holly Anne studied Alexis with a sharp eye. "Any particular reason why?"

She shrugged, not sure what was bothering her, just knowing something was. "Instinct," she said finally.

"Keep working on it. Make this match. And the Galveston office will be yours to run."

And if she didn't, Alexis thought, she'd probably be fresh out of luck, because there was no way the other three partners would vote to put her in charge of the new branch office.

Holly Anne drummed her fingers on the windowsill. "By the way, I had a call from Carolyn Bass...."

Alexis squirmed. "I heard she wants her money back."

The executive's jaw set. "We don't guarantee happily ever after. We deal in possibilities."

"Right."

"It will blow over," Holly Anne promised.

Alexis nodded. She certainly hoped so.

Otherwise, there would be yet another reason she could kiss that promotion and pay raise goodbye....

A rap sounded on her open office door, and both women turned. Grady McCabe stood in the doorway. His dark hair was rumpled, as always, as if he had been running his hands through it. A hint of evening beard rimmed his jaw, giving him a sexy, ruggedly attractive, all-man look. Since she had seen him last, he had changed into a V-necked T-shirt, knee-length shorts and deck shoes appropriate for the hot June evening.

Holly Anne smiled and slid off the corner of Alexis's desk. "I'll let you two converse. See you in the morning."

Alexis nodded as her boss headed for the exit. "Good night."

Grady came closer. The scent of soap and cologne clinging to his skin told her he had recently showered. After a day spent working and running around in the fierce June heat, Alexis yearned to do the same.

"I figured you would be here," he said.

The office was so quiet at this time of night. In the distance, a door shut. Alexis realized she and Grady were completely alone. Playing it cool, she rocked back in her swivel chair. "I thought you'd be with your family."

"Savannah's asleep. Mom and Dad wanted to hit the sack early, too—they were up at dawn checking out drilling sites of my mom's. Not sure if I told you—she's a wildcatter. Runs the oil exploration company she inherited from my grandfather, Big Jim Wyatt. My dad specializes in making money on business investments of all kinds, including but not limited to oil exploration."

Alexis was touched by the affection in his voice. "From what I've heard, they make a good team," she said softly.

One corner of Grady's mouth crooked up. "They met when my mom was drilling for oil on property my dad owned. To hear them tell it, there were a lot of fireworks at first, but then they fell madly in love, married and had five sons."

Alexis watched Grady stroll back and forth, checking out the photos and award plaques on her office walls. She shook her head. "To be the only woman in a family of six men...wow."

Grady grinned. "The testosterone in my family has never overwhelmed my mom. She was a tomboy herself. But the lack of steady women in all her offspring's lives does rankle. She wants all her sons married. And me being the oldest, I'm supposed to do that again ASAP."

Alexis recalled the affectionate way Josie and Wade had interacted. "She wants you to be in love, though."

"You bet." Grady seemed to steel himself. "Which is why I didn't tell my folks about my plan to marry without it."

"So thcy..."

"Still don't know, and I would prefer to keep it that way," he stated flatly.

A less comfortable silence fell between them. Alexis knew Grady thought he wasn't ashamed by his attitude. However, his actions, when it came to his parents, said otherwise. "It is a hard thing to explain," she said eventually.

"It's also the way I feel."

Alexis wished lightning would strike twice. Grady and Savannah deserved to be happy. They deserved to have a complete family, and all the love life had to offer.

"But maybe it can still be good," Grady said, sounding more upbeat than before.

Although her spirits plummeted, she forced herself to smile. "Things went well with Tina?"

Grady's gaze roved over Alexis's pale-blue sheath, his glance lingering on the bare skin of her shoulders, before drifting thoughtfully back to her face. "She left right after you did," he murmured, sounding as if he was suddenly having as much trouble staying on track as she was.

Alexis reminded herself that it was nearly nine o'clock, and had been an exceedingly long day at the end of an exceedingly long week.

"I explained I needed time alone with my family," Grady continued, in a low, matter-of-fact tone.

Without warning, Alexis's heart kicked into a faster beat.

She told herself to calm down. To slip back into matchmaker mode. She looked Grady in the eye, all business once more. "Are you going to see her again?"

His gaze still locked with hers, he shook his head. "I don't think so."

Inexplicably, her heart slowed down once again. Alexis tapped a pen on the surface of her desk. Swallowed. "Any particular reason why?" she asked, surprised how normal her voice could sound, when her emotions were all awhirl.

Grady's lips thinned. "Tina's a very nice person. I think she'd be great with Savannah."

"But?"

"I'm not sure how comfortable I'd be with her."

A feeling akin to relief slid through Alexis. She did not want to match up any other couples who were wrong for each other. She didn't want that on her conscience. Bad enough that Russ and Carolyn Bass were divorcing after just one year…

"I'll let Tina know," Alexis promised.

And when she did so, she'd have another match ready for Tina to consider. A doctor, maybe.

"Thanks."

Alexis reached for the folder on her desk. "Would you like to look at other profiles?"

He paused, and she wasn't sure what he was thinking. Only that he looked conflicted. "How about I take the info with me?" he suggested finally. "And look at it later."

"That would be fine." She gathered up the relevant video interviews and slid them inside the folder, alongside the printed pages, and handed them over.

"Are you done for the day?" Grady asked.

"Yes."

"Walk you out?"

Alexis tried not to think how good that sounded. "Sure."

He waited while she logged off her computer and shut it down. "Want me to carry that?" He indicated the briefcase she had slung over her shoulder.

They were already feeling too much like a couple. And honestly, how ridiculous was that? "That's okay. Thanks."

He strolled beside her, respecting the parameters she'd set. When they reached the elevator, he pushed the down button, then turned to her with a sexy smile. "Have you had dinner?"

"I stopped for a salad on the way back to the office."

His eyes crinkled at the corners. "Bet you didn't have dessert."

"You're right. I did not."

"I know a great French bakery not too far from here that stays open late."

She knew the place he was talking about. The desserts

were to die for. But if she went there with him, they would end up talking, and feeling even closer to each other. Which might have been fine, had they been able to keep their relationship strictly platonic. But they had already proved the hard way that they couldn't do that. They had kissed one another, avidly. And she had the feeling if she went anywhere with him tonight they might end up doing so again.

Which again would have been fine, if they wanted the same things. But they didn't. Which meant she had to stay focused. Find Grady a woman who wouldn't mind being in a loveless marriage—and then move on herself. "Thanks, but..." she had to pause to clear her throat "...I've got other plans."

Big ones. A cold shower. A good book. Another long, lonely night.

His expression inscrutable, he studied her, seeming to know instinctively how much she wished they were on the same page. "Another time then," he said eventually.

She nodded, pretending for cordiality sake that that was so.

They got into the elevator without speaking and he walked her to her car, waited until she was safely inside. "I'll see you at the fund-raiser tomorrow evening," he said in lieu of goodbye.

And that, Alexis noted—trembling slightly as she drove away—was that.

Chapter Six

"Are you going to talk about why you aren't going out this evening?" Josie asked Grady on Saturday as soon as his dad had gone off with Savannah to read bedtime stories.

Grady carried the dirty dishes to the sink. "You and Dad are here."

His mother spritzed spray cleaner across the tabletop. "And you bought a tableful of tickets for the cancer research fund-raising dinner this evening."

From a woman who will be there but does not want to spend time with me, Grady thought.

He opened the dishwasher. "I gave them all to friends."

Josie tore off a paper towel. "I bet you could still get another ticket if you wanted. They'd find a way to fit you in."

Grady imagined that was so. When it came to raising funds for cancer research, every dollar was appreciated.

He watched his mom wipe down the table. "Why would I want to do that?"

She shot him a knowing glance. "Probably the same reason you got cleaned up before heading out last night on 'errands' and came back early."

Grady couldn't deny he had been disappointed at the way

things had turned out. He'd hoped to get to know Alexis better last night, spend a little time together. To what end he wasn't sure—given the fact she'd made it pretty clear she wasn't interested in being "matched" with him. All he knew for certain was that he longed to be with her, surprising as that was... He sent his mother a censuring glance. "I stopped reporting in when I was eighteen."

She ignored his complaint. "What's going on with you and Alexis Graham?"

Grady finished loading the dishwasher, added detergent and shut the door. "What are you talking about?"

Josie tossed the paper towel in the trash. "I haven't seen you look at a woman that way since you met Tabitha."

Grady tensed. The two situations were not the same. They couldn't be. "Just because you were the first to call that romance..." he muttered.

"Does not mean I've lost my intuition around my sons," Josie declared. "I saw the hope in your eyes when you left here last night, and the quiet disappointment in your expression when you returned less than an hour later." She gently touched his arm. "So what's the problem? Is Ms. Graham not interested?"

She's holding out for the kind of love I can't give, Grady thought. *And doesn't want to consider anything else.* And while he was deeply disappointed about that, he couldn't say—in all honesty—that he blamed her. Alexis was the kind of woman who deserved the best life had to offer. Not a pale imitation of the deeply satisfying unions they had both had in the past.

Aware that his mother was still waiting for an answer, he said, "It's a little more complicated than that, Mom. Alexis was married before, too. She lost her husband to cancer a few years ago."

Her expression compassionate, Josie guessed, "So she's not altogether ready to move on, either."

Was that true? Grady recalled the passionate way Alexis had kissed him back, before coming to her senses and ending the embrace. Much as he wanted to forget the way it had felt to hold her in his arms, he couldn't. And his gut told him Alexis couldn't forget *her* attraction to him, either. He shrugged. "Alexis *says* she's open to the idea of getting involved again."

Disappointment resonated in the room. "Just not with you."

Leave it to his mom to hit the nail on the head. "Your sons do strike out from time to time, you know," he reminded her drolly.

Josie grinned. "I know that," she said, rebounding to her usual sunny outlook. "I just would have sworn that wasn't going to be the case in this situation."

AT EIGHT-THIRTY THAT evening, Alexis checked off the final guest stopping by the ticket desk. At last, all the name cards had been picked up. And although Grady McCabe had purchased an entire table, his name had not been on one of the placards, which meant he was not planning to attend.

Given the attraction simmering between them, Alexis should have been relieved she wouldn't see him tonight.

"Well, we did it," Holly Anne, one of the event's organizers, said. "We sold all four hundred and fifty tickets!"

That was a great deal of money, Alexis calculated with satisfaction. It would go a long way toward funding more cancer research.

And hopefully, more lives would be saved. She was very happy about that.

Holly Anne pushed away from the cloth-covered table and regarded Alexis gently. "Scott would be very proud of you—"

"Got room for one more?"

They both turned, to see Grady striding toward them. He looked incredibly handsome in a black tuxedo, pleated white dress shirt and black tie. Alexis's breath caught in her chest. For a second, as their eyes locked and held, time seemed suspended.

Holly Anne greeted him, then turned to Alexis. "I'll let you handle this." She slipped inside the ballroom, shutting the door behind her.

Pulse racing, Alexis looked at Grady. She really should not be so happy to see him tonight. But she was, even though his presence presented yet another dilemma. "Your table—"

"Is full. I know." His gaze swept her from head to foot, obviously taking in her upswept hair and silk halter dress, her silver stilettos and sapphire jewelry. Then he closed the distance between them. "I was hoping I could sit next to you. Assuming you came, as I did, without a date who might object."

She had.

He withdrew a check from his inside jacket pocket and handed it over.

Doing her best to contain her pleasure, she murmured, "Hang on a minute. I'll see what I can do."

Flushing self-consciously, she went off to make the necessary accommodations. She returned to find Grady lounging next to the ballroom doors, looking as if he had all the time in the world.

"They're fitting in an extra place for you now. I have to warn you, though. We have one of the worst tables in the room, at the very back, next to the entrance."

"No place I'd rather be."

She tried not to take his declaration literally. Her spirits rose nevertheless, maybe because he was looking at her as if he was thinking about kissing her again.

Aware the first course was already being served, they slipped inside and found their seats. On the dais, the first guest speaker was recounting his own battle with cancer, the way ongoing research and a clinical trial had saved his life. He was followed by half a dozen more throughout the meal. Listening to the speeches brought it all back to Alexis. More than once she found her eyes welling with tears, of both sadness and joy. Grady—indeed everyone at their table—was similarly touched.

Thanks were given to everyone in attendance, and then the orchestra started up again. His expression compassionate, Grady leaned over to whisper in her ear, "I think you could use a spin on the dance floor."

Alexis knew she needed to do something to ward off the memories crowding in.

Grady took her hand, and she reveled in the warmth and strength of his grip, the callused feeling of his palm.

They were halfway to the dance floor when Lisa Marie Peterson's mother appeared before them.

"Hello, Grady!" she said, ignoring Alexis. "I'm glad you're here tonight. I've been wanting to talk to you about the situation with our little girls."

ALEXIS WOULD HAVE BEEN completely content to let the two parents go off to have their conference alone, but Grady clamped his hand around hers as Kit led the way out of the ballroom, into the corridor. Alexis went along reluctantly.

When Kit finally turned and saw her there, she looked as unhappy as Alexis felt.

But she turned to Grady. "Lisa Marie told me what a nice

apology Savannah gave her. Her father and I are very appreciative."

Alexis noted there was no mention of Kit's daughter's culpability in the brouhaha.

Grady nodded, waiting for whatever was coming next.

The redhead flashed an ingratiating smile. "I just want to let you know there are no hard feelings on our family's part. Savannah will be invited to the mother-daughter tea at our home—the day before kindergarten graduation—like all the other girls in Lisa Marie's class. It'll give them a chance to sit down like the little ladies they are and practice the etiquette they've been learning all year."

"Thanks for letting me know," Grady said, his expression inscrutable.

"I understand this could present a problem for Savannah, bless her heart, since she's the only one in her class who doesn't have a mother…." Kit continued.

Then why do it this way? Alexis wondered. Why design an important end-of-year social event that she knew in advance was only going to make Savannah acutely aware of the deficiency in her young life? Surely there had to be a way to have a tea party without making a child feel ostracized! But then, Alexis thought, going back to the mean girl experiences in her own life, maybe that was the point. To isolate and demean Grady's little girl…so Lisa Marie and her friends would feel better about themselves.

"So," Mrs. Peterson continued brightly, "if you would like to break with tradition and attend along with Savannah, Grady, that would be fine with us."

"Thank you for letting me know that," he repeated, with more politeness than Alexis would have been able to muster, under the same circumstances.

"Naturally," Kit said as she shot an openly condescending

look at Alexis, "we want each child to attend with just one adult, so it won't be possible for you to bring a guest."

Meaning me, or any other female, Alexis thought, not sure why Kit's snub should bother her, only knowing that it did. Maybe, she mused, because her feminine intuition told her that Savannah needed to be protected whenever she was around Lisa Marie and her friends. And the deeply maternal part of her wanted to be there to do it.

Not that this was her job, of course. She knew full well that she wasn't Savannah's mother.

She just felt that way sometimes.

"And now," Kit finished cordially, "I'd like a word with Alexis privately, if I may."

Alexis could tell Grady didn't want her conversing with Kit Peterson. She didn't want to have a tête-à-tête with the stunning redhead, either. Unfortunately, as a member of the event committee, she could hardly say no. Especially since she had no idea what this was about. "How can I help you?" She asked, as the two of them walked a short distance down the corridor, to an alcove around the corner.

Without Grady there for an audience, Kit dispensed with the saccharine smile and got straight to the point. "I heard you're looking for a new mother for Savannah."

Alexis reluctantly confirmed what was now, thanks to the brawl that had landed Savannah in the principal's office, common knowledge around Miss Chilton's Academy for Young Women. "I work for ForeverLove.com." And that was all the information Alexis was going to give.

Excitement gleamed in Kit's eyes. "Well, look no further. A friend of mine—Zoe Borden—is perfect for Grady."

Alexis put up a silencing hand and stated firmly, "I can't discuss clients."

Kit stepped closer. "You need to call me," she said urgently. "Between the two of us, we can set something up."

No, we can't, Alexis thought, as a shadow loomed in her peripheral vision.

They turned to see Grady. Seeming to realize they were close to what Alexis guessed would be a vehement disagreement—at least on Kit's side—he planted his palm on the small of Alexis's back and brought her in close to his side, his manner as resolute as it was protective. "Alexis, your presence is requested inside the ballroom."

She had an idea who wanted her there. And he was standing right beside her.

"Enjoy the rest of your evening," Grady told Kit deliberately.

Clearly taken aback, the redhead nodded curtly and flounced off.

"What was that about?" he asked, when the two of them were alone once again.

Alexis shrugged off the near-unpleasantness. "The usual." *More or less,* she added silently to herself. "She heard I was a matchmaker."

A hint of devilry came into Grady's blue eyes. "Let me guess. She has a friend who is looking to get married."

And not just to anyone, Alexis thought sarcastically. Out loud, she affirmed, "Something like that."

"Are you going to help her?"

Alexis couldn't imagine any friend of Kit Peterson's would be right for Grady. She shook her head. "If her friend signs up with the agency, she'll be given to someone else. I have my hands full right now with the clients I have."

"I've heard one of 'em is nothing but trouble," Grady teased.

No kidding, Alexis thought, her heart fluttering once again. Already, she wanted to kiss him. And if she kissed him, she was going to want to kiss him again, and if she did that... She really couldn't go there, even in her thoughts.

Alexis held her ground with effort. "There's trouble," she said lightly, "and then there's trouble with a capital T." Grady fell into the latter category. Worse, he seemed to know it.

Still grinning, he took her hand once again. "About that dance..."

Alexis knew that if he held her in his arms, the chemistry she felt whenever she was near him would ignite into a dangerous desire. Life had already dealt her enough heartache without her voluntarily signing up for more. She called on every bit of willpower she had, took a deep, bolstering breath and withdrew her tingling hand from his. "You're a client, Grady. I shouldn't be dancing with you."

His smile faded. "You were willing before."

Still was, if the truth be known... Coolly, she responded, "Only because you didn't give me a chance to say no."

He studied her perceptively. "And now that you've had time to think about it...?"

Alexis pushed aside her romantic fantasies and forced herself to come to her senses. One of them had to be practical. It looked as if it was going to be her. Doing her best to erect another wall between them, she said, "Our becoming close can only get in the way of what I'm trying to do for you and Savannah."

Grady's dark brows drew together. "And dancing together would accomplish that?"

Alexis gave him a withering look. "What do you think?"

"STRUCK OUT AGAIN, hmm?" Wade McCabe asked, when Grady walked in shortly after eleven.

He hadn't had this much commentary on his love life or

lack thereof when he had been in his teens. Ignoring the frustration and disappointment roiling in his gut, he tossed his father a droll look. "I thought you'd be asleep by now."

His dad grinned, not about to be diverted. "Your mother is."

Knowing a heart-to-heart was in the offing, Grady grabbed the open container of orange juice from the fridge.

"Your mother is worried about you," his father continued.

Grady uncapped the plastic jug, lifted it to his lips and drank the half cup or so that was left. "She worries about all her kids, all the time."

Wade watched as Grady wiped his mouth with the back of his hand. "You especially. She thinks that, apart from the time you spend with Savannah, you aren't enjoying life the way you should."

Grady tossed the empty container in the recycling bin. As long as they were talking honestly… He looked his father in the eye. "There hasn't been a whole lot to be happy about, beside my kid and job success."

His dad put the lid on the tin of cookies on the counter. "Maybe this matchmaking service will work out. At least help you get back in the game, if you know what I mean."

And maybe it wouldn't, Grady thought.

All he knew was that Alexis had been working on his situation for almost a week now, and he was no closer to finding a mother for his daughter.

He also knew that he was lonelier than ever.

Fortunately, he had a lot of work to do. And since his parents were going to be in town until Monday morning, now was a chance to get caught up.

HE WAS ELBOW DEEP in the latest cost projections the following afternoon when his cell phone rang.

A burst of pleasure warmed his chest when he saw the caller ID flash across the screen. Lifting the phone to his ear, he found his smile broaden as a soft sexy voice rippled through the receiver. "Grady?"

"Hey, Alexis." He rocked back in his chair.

"Is this a good time?" she asked.

"The best," Grady said. "What's up?"

She continued in the gentle, businesslike voice he had come to know and appreciate. "I've compiled another list of potential mates for you. I wanted to drop by and give them to you." She paused.

He could picture her scraping her teeth across her lower lip....

"I thought—hoped—because it was the weekend you might have a chance to look at them and give me your opinion, so I could get dates set up for you every day this week. But if you're busy with family..."

Despite his own resolve to provide a mommy for his little girl, the idea of dating was no more appealing than it had been at the outset. Nevertheless, he knew he had to keep trying. Savannah needed a woman in her life.

Grady turned his chair so he could look out over downtown Fort Worth. As always on a Sunday afternoon, the streets were quiet, with only the occasional car or pickup driving by. "I'm at the office. My parents took Savannah for the day. So if you want to drop them by—"

"I'll be right over. Thanks, Grady." *Click.*

Twenty minutes later, building security called to let him know that Alexis was on her way up to see him. Grady met her at the elevator and walked her through the deserted executive suite to his private office.

He was painfully aware he could have done more in the

grooming department today—he had showered, but not shaved. Put on a faded burnt-orange-and-white Texas alumni T-shirt with an ink stain across the hem, jeans and running shoes.

Not that she seemed to mind.

He shut the door behind them. Gestured for her to take a seat. Took a moment to survey her as she got settled.

Her silky hair was caught in a clip on the back of her head. She was dressed casually—in a pale pink sundress, a thin white silk cardigan and flat-heeled sandals with a rose in the center of the thin straps across her feet.

He had never seen her bare feet, he realized. They were small and delicate, the toenails polished a sexy hot pink. Her legs were bare and smooth, without the usual panty hose....

She leaned forward to open up the carryall that served as both purse and briefcase, extracted a sheath of papers and half a dozen DVDs bearing the company logo.

It was only when she straightened and looked him square in the face that he noticed the faint puffiness around her eyes.

TOO LATE, Alexis realized the makeup she had applied so carefully before leaving her apartment had not done the trick.

"What's wrong?" Grady asked. He came back around the desk.

It had been a mistake coming here today. Thinking work—and possibly, time spent with Grady—would erase her overwhelming sense of loss and grief. "If you're talking about my eyes..."

"It looks like you've been crying."

"It's allergies," Alexis fibbed. Deciding to just hand the information over and flee while the going was good, she stood.

"Bull. It's something else, if your eyes are that swollen."

"I don't want to talk about it." The words were no sooner

out than the tears began to well once again. The next thing she knew his arms were around her, hauling her against him. While her tears fell in a river, dampening his shirt, he stroked her hair, saying nothing. But then, nothing needed to be said.

Alexis struggled to get ahold of herself once again. She pulled away from him and rubbed the moisture from her cheeks. "I don't know what's wrong with me today," she murmured, averting her gaze.

He studied her closely. "It's because of last night. Something the speakers said…"

What had been meant to be uplifting had brought up everything she wished never to think about again. Suddenly, she couldn't hold it all in anymore.

In a choked voice, she cried, "I just wish it had never happened!" She looked in Grady's eyes and saw understanding. Like it or not, they were both in a club no one ever wanted to join. "I wish that Scott had never gotten sick or suffered the way he did, or had his life taken away from him."

Knowing Grady had lost a spouse, too, gave her the courage to admit, "I wish we'd had a chance to have the children we wanted. Although…" Alexis's lips curved ruefully "…seeing Savannah deal with the loss of a parent makes me realize how selfish that is."

"It's okay to want kids," he said compassionately. "It's okay to want things to be different. But at the same time…" he shrugged "…you've got to know our lives are what they are…."

And nothing they said or did would change that.

Alexis relaxed slightly. "Usually, I can deal."

"Then what was different about yesterday?" Grady asked, edging closer.

She reveled in the warmth of his nearness. "It was the anniversary of Scott's diagnosis."

Grady nodded, as if knowing firsthand that the date life as you knew it had screeched to a halt was always hard to bear. It didn't matter how much time passed.

Alexis gulped. "I thought by being involved in the fundraiser this year I would be able to turn the day our lives went all to hell into something good, really start moving on… instead of being stuck in what was…."

Grady stroked a hand through her hair. He looked as if he approved of her decision to move on—and why not, since he was attempting to do the same thing? "You could start by taking a day off every now and then."

Alexis scoffed. "You're one to talk!"

He favored her with a sexy half smile. "I took yesterday off."

"So did I."

"You worked a benefit—I wouldn't call that time off. I'm talking about time to just be."

He had no idea how good that sounded.

Alexis focused on the strong column of Grady's throat. She splayed her hands across his chest and felt the steady beat of his heart beneath her fingertips. "I wish it was that simple." But it wasn't. For starters, the two of them, though wildly attracted to each other, did not want the same things. She had to keep remembering that.

As for the rest…

Alexis sighed.

Grady sifted his hands through her hair, lifted her face up to his. "Why isn't it that easy?"

He wouldn't understand unless she told him. And suddenly she wanted him to know at least this much about her. "I need to work every second I can because I'm up to my neck in debt." It was why she lived in a less-than-ideal apartment instead of a house, and drove a company-leased car. When his brow furrowed, she explained, "Insurance only funded a portion of the cancer treatment, and Scott battled leukemia for two years. Luckily, his co-pays were capped at twenty-one thousand a year, but that's still forty-two thousand dollars, plus another twelve thousand for his funeral, and countless other expenses, like hospital parking fees and lost wages."

She took in a quavering breath. "Suffice it to say, I'll be paying off that debt for a very long time. Unless I get the job running the new Galveston office, and the increase in salary that comes with it. Then it will happen a lot sooner, of course."

Grady was silent, looking down at her with compassion. "I wish I could help."

She knew he was rich. Did he think she was asking him for money…?

Oh God, no.

Embarrassed she had told him so much about the private details of her life, Alexis stepped back abruptly. "It's not your problem." And it wouldn't be.

Suddenly, she needed to get out of there as soon as possible, and head back to work. She grabbed her carryall, slung it over her shoulder. "Let me know what you think about the candidates so I can set something up as soon as possible."

He studied her closely. "Meet me at the Reata Restaurant at seven o'clock," he said. "We'll go over it, and I'll tell you what I think then."

NOT SURE WHY she'd agreed to have dinner with Grady when she could just as easily gotten the information from him over the phone, Alexis went back to her own office. She spent the rest of the afternoon tending to several other clients, and pulling up another half dozen files, just in case Grady did not like any of the six women she had profiled for him. She went straight to the restaurant from work.

He was there, waiting for her. Dressed in a sage-green dress shirt, khaki pants and boots. He had shaved since she had seen him last, and put on aftershave. Suddenly, this felt like a date.

It shouldn't.

Marshalling her defenses, she slid into the chair he held out for her. "Well?" she said brightly, reminding herself she had handled much tougher situations than seeing a guy she was secretly attracted to pick someone else, at her urging. "What did you decide?"

"The kindergarten teacher, Pauline Emory. On paper, she sounds perfect."

That was depressingly easy. Alexis kept her hurt feelings to herself. "That's what I thought, too," she agreed cordially, rummaging through her notebook so she wouldn't have to look Grady in the eye. "I would have recommended her sooner, but she just signed on Friday, so her information wasn't in the system yet. Anyway, I'll call her and set something up." Unable to help but feel disappointed that their business had been concluded so swiftly—she'd been looking forward to having dinner with Grady, even if it was strictly business—she reached for her carryall and started to rise.

Grady caught her wrist. It was his turn to look flustered. "Where are you going?" he asked in surprise.

"Well..." Alexis tried not to focus on the intimate feel of his skin on hers. "We don't need to have dinner," she said, feeling as if her heart would bolt right out of her chest. "Our business is concluded."

His grasp tightened protectively. “Not quite.” Grady caught the eye of a man sitting at the bar.

Alexis’s eyes widened. Why was Grady’s father here?

Wade McCabe strolled over to join them. “Hello, Alexis.”

Completely dumbfounded, she nodded. “Mr. McCabe.” Alexis turned back to Grady. “What’s going on?” His father couldn’t want the services of a matchmaker! He was already married. Why hadn’t Grady mentioned that his father would be joining them?

“Grady told me about your situation,” he stated affably, as he pulled up a chair.

“You already indicated you didn’t want my help,” Grady explained.

Wade nodded and flashed her a genial grin. “So we were hoping you’d accept mine.”

Chapter Seven

"C'mon, Alexis! Talk to me!" Grady called through the closed apartment door a short time later.

He could hear her stomping around the small space, obviously angry and insulted. "Go away, Grady!" she shouted back.

The door behind him opened, and Alexis's neighbor, a short and burly Latino man, stared ominously at him.

"This guy bothering you?" he shouted.

The door to Alexis's flat swung open. Jaw working, she planted her hands on her slender hips and stared at them both. "No," she told her neighbor. Her face softened in appreciation. "Thanks, Augusto."

The man surveyed her a moment longer. "Then keep it down, will you?" he said gruffly at last. "The baby is asleep."

"Right." Alexis nodded, contritely. "Sorry."

He then glared at Grady, as if expecting him to leave.

Grady looked at Alexis.

She appeared to be weighing her options, then exhaled loudly and motioned him in. "You've got two minutes to speak your piece," she snapped.

"You call me if you need me," Augusto stated.

"Thank you." Alexis looked warningly at Grady. "But it won't be necessary."

He followed her inside.

The first thing he noticed was how small her place was. Located in an area known for housing young families, the efficiency rented—according to the sign outside—for six hundred a month, utilities not included. She had a window unit air conditioner, which, although noisy, seemed to be putting out plenty of cool air. A worn tweed sofa bed was unfolded for sleeping, and there was a table with one chair for eating, a small desk with the other chair for working. The door to a tiny bathroom was ajar, and he glimpsed an ancient pedestal sink inside. The kitchen held an under-counter dorm-style refrigerator, microwave and hot plate. No dishwasher or disposal.

One entire wall of the flat was taken up with books, another with racks of neatly maintained and organized clothes and shoes. He wasn't surprised about that. Her line of business demanded she dress nicely, when interacting with clients.

The portable TV in the corner was tuned to a popular home decorating show. She snapped it off. "You've got one minute and a half," she said.

The clock was ticking. "Why did you walk out of the restaurant like that?" he asked.

She crossed her arms in front of her. "Because the meeting was over."

They faced off in silence. "Obviously, I offended you."

"Duh." She glowered at him, letting him know with a searing glance how humiliated and embarrassed she had been. *"You think?"*

It was a good thing he liked a challenge. "I was trying to help."

She propped her fists on her hips, her feet planted slightly apart. "I do not need you or anyone in your family to loan me money to consolidate my debts."

"My dad wasn't going to loan you the money himself," Grady told Alexis calmly. "He was simply going to underwrite it, the same way he does for any business or person he's interested in investing in, so the bank would issue you one at a premium interest rate."

Grady was disappointed to see that the distinction did not win him any points with her.

"I'm sure your father's heart was in the right place, Grady," Alexis stated carefully, "but I don't need his help any more than I need yours."

Grady thought about the crushing debt she had described. "This—" he gestured to the five-hundred-square-foot living area, which seemed in many ways as joyless as his own life had been after his wife's death "—tells me otherwise."

"I'm fine."

Was she? "You deserve better."

Alexis angled her chin. "And I'll get it without anyone's help or interference, when I've paid off my debts."

"Anyone ever tell you that you're stubborn to a fault?"

Anger flashed in her eyes. "Anyone ever tell you that you're clueless to a fault?"

His parents had tried. They'd both felt it was a bad idea to make the offer. Grady had convinced them otherwise. And because they liked Alexis, they'd agreed to go along with it…even as they shook their heads and predicted disaster.

"I was just trying to help you out, one friend to another."

"Really." She shoved a hand through her hair. "And how many other 'friends' of one week have you offered to loan upwards of seventy-five thousand dollars to even through a third party?"

Silence fell between them again.

He noticed she had taken off her thin sweater. The sundress she was wearing had a figure-hugging bodice and spaghetti straps, one of which had fallen down her shoulder.

Reluctantly, he tore his eyes from the expanse of bare, silky skin.

The relationship that only hours before had seemed so full of possibilities now seemed like a metaphor for the confused state of his life.

"That's not the kind of thing a guy does for a female friend—it's the kind of thing a man does for his mistress or *potential* mistress."

That woke Grady up. He stared at her. "Excuse me!"

"You heard me! That's the kind of move that typically comes with strings attached—if not sooner, then later."

The idea that she could even for one red-hot second imagine him that calculating and crass, rankled. "You think I went to all that trouble because I wanted to sleep with you?" he asked incredulously, watching the play of emotions across her face.

Alexis swallowed, looking almost sorry she'd brought it up. But now that she had, she was obviously not about to back away from the rash statement. "Maybe not consciously…but yeah," she blurted. "I think romancing me is in the back of your mind!"

Grady stepped closer, purposely invading her physical space. "Then I guess you missed the part where I told you, when you interviewed me about my revised requirements in a potential wife, that I had no interest in having a romantic relationship!"

Alexis scoffed. "Oh, no! I got that!" She thrust her index finger at him. "And I have to tell you, it hasn't exactly made my job of matching you with a woman any easier! I also got the part where you kissed me like there was no tomorrow. The part where I realized that although you may want a mother for Savannah, what you're really looking for here—for yourself—is a friend with benefits! And I have to tell you, you're not the first to present me with that option!"

The idea of Alexis being treated as anything less than the wonderful woman she was filled Grady with fury. He stared at her in shock. "You've been propositioned before?"

She didn't answer right away, but then she didn't have to, as a mixture of rueful recollection and bitterness filled her eyes. "What is it about guys and heartbroken widows, huh? What makes them think that we're all just begging to be bedded? That being crazy with grief equates to being crazy with lust? Because I have to tell you that hasn't been the case with me."

The same as it was with him. When it came to him and her… It was a very different story. He wasn't going to let her pretend otherwise, and group him with every other selfish jerk who had tried to make a move on her.

Alexis wasn't just a conquest to him. She was a person. Flesh and blood, with the heart and soul of a woman, who was every bit as lonely—and in need of companionship—as he was.

"I don't want to be intimately involved with anyone right now," she declared. "Casually or otherwise."

He wasn't just anyone. He was someone who had suffered the same kind of crushing loss she had. Like it or not, that gave them a unique bond. Drawing on that rapport, he said softly, "I thought you said you wanted to marry again someday."

She flinched, for a moment looking as vulnerable as she had that afternoon in his office. "*Someday* being the operative word," she answered quietly.

Grady would have accepted that declaration had the present not been filled with such incredible chemistry.

"And you know why?" she added. Her eyes glimmered as she glanced at him. "Because I haven't given up on having it all."

Grady figured he had—and with good reason. The odds were stacked against either of them ever finding that kind of love again. But he also realized life was too short to let the passion they were experiencing—even here and now as they argued—slide by. He knew better than most that life could change in an instant. All anyone ever really had was the present. And in this moment of time, there was only one thing…only one person…he wanted.

He gave in to a whim and lifted the strap that had fallen down her arm back onto her shoulder, then let his hand slide beneath her hair to the nape of her neck. Luxuriating in the silky feel of her skin, he tilted her face up to his. The way she looked at him then, all soft and wanting, prodded him to risk even more. "The kiss you gave me the other night said otherwise."

Alexis's lips compressed. She lowered her lashes and retorted in a low, unsteady voice, "That kiss was ill-advised."

"Sometimes ill-advised is what's called for," Grady said, aware that his heart was suddenly slamming against his ribs. And then he did what he'd been wanting to do ever since the first time they'd embraced. He guided Alexis closer and slanted his lips over hers, taking everything she had to give.

Grady hadn't come here for this, but he couldn't say he was sorry it was happening. Instinct told him she needed this—needed him—as much as he needed her. Something about feeling her pressed against him, reaching for him, made him come alive. Made him want to connect with her in the most intimate of ways.

Basking in the gentle surrender of her body, he kissed her deeply. As he inhaled the sweet scent of her skin and the lingering fragrance of her perfume, he knew he'd been resurrected at long last. No longer moving numbly through his days, he was totally immersed in the here and now. The warmth of her touch. The womanly taste of her tongue. The softness of her breasts brushing up against his chest. Blood thundered through his body.

She was on tiptoe now, wrapping her arms around his neck, threading her hands through his hair. Her hips pressed against his, and still it wasn't enough….

"Alexis…" It was an effort to get the words out. "If I stay…" he warned, retaining control with effort.

"I know what will happen, Grady," she whispered back, looking deep into his eyes. Every emotion was stripped bare, yet her gaze never wavered. "I want this, too."

And tonight, wanting was all it took….

With the intoxicating scent of her filling his senses, he guided her backward to the sofa bed. "Then show me," he demanded gruffly.

And that, as it turned out, was all the encouragement she needed.

Alexis ran her hands across his shoulders, down his spine. Fused her mouth to his, stroking his tongue with hers. Until all he could think about, all he could feel, was the way her firm body fitted against him. Through the thin fabric of her sundress, her nipples beaded against the muscles of his chest.

Impatient, he slipped a hand beneath her and eased the zipper down, past her hips. He drew away the bodice, revealing a pale yellow, strapless bra. Her pink, jutting nipples were visible through the transparent lace. Lust poured through him, along with something else a lot more difficult to quantify. The need to touch...more than just her body. The need to possess...more than just her momentary will.

Reassuring himself this was only physical, he dipped his head, kissing the swell of her breasts through the cloth. With a low moan of pleasure, she arched her back, offering herself up to him, with a purity and innocence that rocked him to his core. Refusing to acknowledge how much this would have meant to both of them under other circumstances, he pushed the dress lower, past her navel, over her thighs.

Her panties, in the same pale yellow, were cut high on the thigh, revealing an expanse of fair, smooth skin. Pulse racing, he dispensed with the dress, slid his hands beneath her hips and lifted her to him. "Incredible," he murmured, loving the way she opened herself up to him.

And then she was shifting, pushing him back, rising up to kneel beside him. Still clad in panties and bra, she reached for the buttons on his shirt. His belt. His fly. Minutes later, he was naked. Seconds after that, she was, too. "Protection," she murmured.

He stopped as reality crashed upon them once again. "I don't suppose..."

She shook her head.

Aching, but no less determined to have her, he said, "So we won't do that." Eyes locked with hers, he drew Alexis back down beside him. Wrapping an arm around her trembling body, he draped her thigh over his and guided her against him for a long, leisurely kiss. "There are other ways...." he promised.

The last thing Alexis had expected to be doing was lying naked with Grady on her bed, making out like two teenagers, but as they continued to kiss and caress each other, the frustration at their lack of foresight was replaced by a steadily building pleasure.

Grady was right. There were other ways to be close.

Ways that felt just as good. Just as satisfying. He hadn't just led her into a firestorm of heat. Grady knew how to touch her, how to caress her just so, how to make her feel as if she was the only woman on earth for him. And her own instinct was just as strong. Before she knew it, the pleasure was soaring out of control. She was coming apart, and so was he. He caught her to him. Their hearts thundered in unison. Together, they climaxed, and just as slowly and inevitably, drifted back to earth.

ALEXIS'S EYES WERE CLOSED. Grady was not entirely sure that was a good sign. He wished to hell he'd had a condom with him. A box of them. But the truth was, it had been so long since he'd been with someone he hadn't even thought about it. He kissed her shoulder, making a mental note to stop by the drugstore at the first available opportunity so they wouldn't be limited to a hot and heavy make-out session. "Next time…I'll have more foresight," he murmured.

Alexis stiffened.

Obviously, Grady thought, the wrong thing to say.

She pushed him away and sat up. "There isn't going to be a next time, Grady."

O-kay. Maybe, under the circumstances, he should have expected this. Still, being iced out only moments after love-making was a kick in the groin…. He watched her grab the blanket and wrap it around her, toga-style. "Mind telling me why?" He forced himself to sound casual as she disappeared into the tiny bathroom.

She came out seconds later, wrapped in a pink, jersey knit

robe that clung to her slender curves with just enough accuracy to get him hard again. "Because we don't love each other."

What could he say to that? Grady wondered, tearing his eyes from the hint of breast exposed in the V neckline. Except what he had already repeated to Alexis and every other woman who had crossed his path since his wife died? He steeled himself against unnecessary complications. "That's not in the equation for me." He didn't want to be hurt like that again. Didn't want to hope that this time it would be different—this love would last. It felt too much like tempting fate.

She sat down next to him on the bed, looking impossibly composed for a woman who had just given herself to him with no reservation. "I know that. You were perfectly clear on the topic from the very beginning."

"So?" His frustration mounted.

She turned away. "So this was cathartic, in that neither of us has been with anyone in a very long time."

Too long, Grady was beginning to conclude. Otherwise, he would have done the smart thing and kept their relationship platonic, so the two of them could remain friends.

"Don't get me wrong. I enjoyed it," she admitted. "But it can't happen again."

ALEXIS WASN'T SURE how she did it—behaved as if her whole world was not crashing down around her. But somehow she got Grady dressed and out of there in record time.

When the door closed behind him, she went back to her rumpled bed. She had turned the window unit on high when she came home, and cool air was still blasting out of it. Shivering, she climbed beneath the covers and closed her eyes. The overwhelming guilt she expected, at having made the first real attempt to move on after her husband's death, was nowhere to be found.

For the first time in a very long time, there was no sorrow. There wasn't really even any loneliness. There was just the warmth of their bodies, still in the covers. The smell of Grady—that unique mixture of soap, man and aftershave lotion—mingled with the muskier scent of their love.

Thinking about the unabashed way they had pleasured each other filled her entire body with heat. She couldn't believe they had gone at it like teenagers. That she had very nearly risked pregnancy and more, for a moment's pleasure with a man she knew in her mind—if not her heart—was all wrong for her.

Instead, all she had been able to think was about the way he made her feel. So completely, wonderfully alive. So impatient for more. For the first time since she could remember, she was ready to get on with her life.

She wanted, she realized belatedly, to put an end to the long, lonely nights. She wanted someone to talk to. She wanted children. She wanted a real home, with a yard, and a backyard swing, instead of the cheapest apartment she could find.

She wanted Grady.

It was just too bad he wasn't available. Not the way she needed him to be.

ALEXIS DIDN'T HEAR FROM Grady McCabe again that night. She told herself it was for the best. She had asked him to leave. His parents were still in town. Tomorrow was a school day....

Still, when Monday morning dawned, and she received a short e-mail indicating that he still intended to meet with kindergarten teacher Pauline Emory for breakfast, as scheduled, Alexis breathed a sigh of relief.

Or at least she told herself it was relief, not despair. What had she expected? That one hot and heavy tryst would lead him to some great epiphany about wanting romance and commitment, after all?

Telling herself to grow up, she dressed and went to the office. No sooner had Alexis booted up her computer than her boss strode in. "How's it going with Grady McCabe?" she asked.

Alexis pushed the image of Grady making love to her from her mind. She forced a smile. "He's seeing a potential candidate this morning."

Holly Anne frowned. "You're usually so quick to find the perfect someone for a client. I was hoping you'd have Grady matched by now."

Same here. The less time I spend with the sexy heartbreaker, the better...

Alexis struggled to keep her emotions under wraps. "It's not a typical case. Usually romance is involved."

"He's rich. Successful. Handsome. He has an adorable daughter in desperate need of a mommy. How hard can it be to get women lined up to marry him?"

"Not difficult at all." *Sad to say.* Alexis was disappointed at how many women were perfectly willing to throw love out the window, if they could have everything else.

She took a sip of iced coffee. "The problem is Grady. He's proving very difficult to please."

Holly Anne checked her messages on her BlackBerry. "How many clients has he met thus far?"

"Pauline Emory is the third," Alexis replied.

Her boss sent a text and looked up. "That's not so bad, is it?"

"It wouldn't be if he weren't in such a hurry." *If I hadn't lost all sense of propriety and succumbed to him.* Alexis gulped and pretended to look at her computer screen. "He wants this wrapped up in the next two weeks."

"Or sooner," a familiar male voice said, "given the fact that Savannah's summer break starts July first, and I'm going to need someone by then."

Well, if it wasn't the man of the hour.

Doing the best to ignore the jump in her pulse, Alexis glanced at her watch as Grady strode in the door. "I thought you were supposed to be with Pauline Emory."

If he was thinking about the passion that had flared between them the last time they'd seen each other, Alexis thought, he was definitely not showing it. "I met with her after I dropped Savannah off at school," he said.

"And?" Alexis prodded.

Grady flashed an inscrutable smile that did not reach his eyes. "Pauline's great," he said, his tone devoid of emotion. "I think Savannah will like her. Her experience as a kindergarten teacher should help her connect with my daughter."

"Good. I'm glad." Lamenting her sudden hoarseness, Alexis reached for her iced coffee and took another long sip. What was wrong with her? She was supposed to feel happy about his interest in Pauline, not sad and rejected.

Grady continued matter-of-factly, "Pauline's off for the summer—she teaches at a school on the regular calendar—so I asked her to tutor Savannah after school every day for the next week and a half. See if she can't get Savannah enthused about doing her homework, so it's not such a hassle."

Tutoring wasn't exactly the same as dating with a view toward marriage, Alexis thought. She could tell that Holly Anne was having the same troubled reaction. "And Pauline agreed?"

Grady's contained expression told Alexis that Pauline Emory hadn't exactly been thrilled about it. He shrugged his broad shoulders. "She understands I'm doing this for Savannah, not for me."

So nothing had changed, Alexis realized pensively. Grady was still keeping every woman who was interested in him at arm's length. He was only looking for a suitable mother for his daughter. And while that might work in the short run, she knew it would not work in the long run. Unfortunately, it wasn't her decision to make. Her job was to cater to Grady's whims.

"In the meantime, do you want me to keep presenting you with other candidates?"

Grady shook his head. "Not until I see whether this works out."

It sounded as if he was getting serious, Alexis noted with alarm.

"I can only juggle one potential wife at a time," Grady said flatly.

Which means I'm out of the picture entirely, Alexis thought with a sinking heart. *Not that I was ever* in *the picture...except as a means to an end.*

She forced herself to meet his gaze. "That's good to know."

Holly Anne beamed, obviously seeing this as progress. "Sounds like you'll be in Galveston before you know it," she whispered to Alexis.

Seeing her secretary appear in the doorway, Holly Anne asked, "Problem?" At the answering nod, she hurried out.

Once again Grady and Alexis were alone. A brief, uncomfortable silence fell between them. Finally, he raised his brow. "Are congratulations in order?"

Was it her imagination or was there the faintest hint of concern—and maybe even disappointment—in his eyes?

She shrugged self-consciously to let him know any such talk was way premature. "I haven't been offered the job. The four partners still have to vote on it at the end of the month." And there was no way of telling how that would go, particularly if Grady remained as hard to please. ForeverLove.com was an agency that prided itself on *results.* Unsatisfied customers hurt—not helped—profits. Holly Anne and her partners were all about the bottom line.

As was Grady, apparently, Alexis noted.

"Will you take it if offered the position?" he asked her casually.

Pack up and move several hundred miles away? A week ago, thinking the change of pace, not to mention the extra money, would be helpful to her, Alexis would have said yes unequivocally. Now?

Honestly, she didn't know.

But if she told Grady so he'd think she was only staying in Fort Worth because of him.

And if he thought that, he'd think she was ripe for a continuation of their never-to-be-repeated encounter.

She wasn't.

So, for both their sakes, she told him what she knew he least wanted to hear, even though she was no longer sure the statement was accurate. "From a financial standpoint, I'd be a fool not to."

Chapter Eight

"Grady?" Pauline Emory paused in the door of his study. "We've got a bit of a problem." She glided on in, looking every bit the suburban mom. Smart, energetic, friendly, the slender brunette was everything most Texas men would want in a potential wife.

Except him.

Despite her many laudable qualities, when he looked at her, all he could see was what she wasn't. Namely, Alexis.

If only Alexis were willing to settle for what he could give her…instead of what he *couldn't.*

But she didn't want to settle.

And he couldn't pretend he would ever believe in happily-ever-after again.

Grady sighed, forcing himself to listen to what Pauline was saying as she paused next to his desk, the bangle bracelet sliding down her wrist, drawing his attention to her expertly manicured hands.

Which was another thing he didn't like, Grady thought.

Acrylic nails.

"We've been at this for over an hour now…." Pauline heaved a distressed sigh. "Savannah absolutely refuses to finish her homework. She said she can't do it."

Not couldn't, Grady thought. Wouldn't. He looked at Pauline, recalling from the file he'd read on her that she had twice been named Teacher of the Year at the elementary school where she worked. He lifted a brow. "Surely—"

Pauline cut him off. "I've tried every pre-k method I know. She's not budging."

No one had to tell him how stubborn his daughter could be, especially when she had it in her mind not to cooperate. Grady pushed away from his computer keyboard, lamenting the fact that his plan had already hit the skids. He headed for the door. "Where is she?"

"On the swing set." Pauline touched his arm before he could get past the portal. "Listen, I think I should go," she said gently.

This was a surprise.

"Savannah's in no mood to spend time with anyone new today. I don't think we should push it. Maybe just try again tomorrow. With the three of us."

That wasn't what Grady had had in mind. He could see Pauline had reached her limit, however. He walked her to the front door. "I'll call you later," he said.

She smiled. "I'm sure Savannah will do better if it's the three of us," she repeated.

Or not, Grady thought.

He said goodbye and headed to the backyard.

Savannah was sitting on the swing. She was still in her school uniform. Surprised that she hadn't changed into one of her princess costumes, as was usually the case, Grady leaned against the tall wooden post just to the right of her. He shoved his hands in the pockets of his trousers. "What's going on?" he inquired.

Savannah looked up at him. "I want Alexis," she said.

"WHAT'S GOING ON?" Alexis asked Grady, the moment she arrived. She had been on her way home from the office when she got the message that he had some sort of emergency at his home and needed to see her ASAP. "Where's Pauline?"

"She left." Briefly, Grady explained.

"You don't look thrilled," Alexis noted.

"To be truthful, I'm not sure it's going to work out with her. She and Savannah didn't really seem to hit it off. Not the way the two of you did. And that kind of rapport is what I'm looking for."

Alexis couldn't blame him. Anything less would not hold up over time. "How'd the tutoring go?"

"Terrible. Savannah wouldn't cooperate. Pauline gave up and went home."

Alexis made a face. That wasn't good. "How much did they get done?"

"Not one problem. Which is why I sent out the SOS to you. Savannah said only *you* could help her with her math."

Alexis shook her head in silent remonstration. She propped her hands on her hips as the mood between them lightened considerably. "And you fell for that?"

A guilty-as-charged-but-so-glad-to-see-you grin tugged at the corners of Grady's lips. "You're always so good with her," he answered wryly.

Not exactly a reason to set her heart to pounding. Although, Alexis admitted reluctantly to herself, it felt kind of good to know that Savannah missed her as much as she missed the little girl. And, truth be told, it warmed her heart that when in trouble, Grady didn't hesitate to call. She hadn't been needed—or wanted—like that in someone's life since her husband died.

"Alexis!" Savannah came running into the room. She was still in her school uniform and a pair of purple cowgirl boots, a tiara perched precariously on her head. "Daddy, you didn't tell me Alexis was here! Where've you been? How come you didn't come and see me? Do you want to go upstairs and play Fairy Princess?"

Alexis grinned—she couldn't help it. Knowing full well she shouldn't be encouraging this "little diva" behavior, she wrapped her arms around Grady's daughter and returned her exuberant embrace. "I've been very busy working, sweetheart."

Still holding on tight, Savannah looked up at her. "Did you miss me as much as I missed you?"

"Yes," Alexis told her sincerely. "Very much."

Savannah beamed.

"I hear you have homework to do," she continued gently.

The child collapsed to the floor dramatically, then brought her arms and legs in close to her torso, resting her chin on her upraised knees. "I can't do it today," she said, suddenly looking distressed and completely overwhelmed. "I'm too upset."

Alexis knelt down beside her. "About what, honey?"

"I don't have a dress for graduation."

Grady looked stunned. "I thought you were wearing your school uniforms to graduation."

Savannah shook her head, more distraught than ever. "No, Daddy," she explained with exaggerated patience. "My teacher said we all have to wear party dresses."

Grady shrugged, clearly not getting the importance. "Well, that's no problem. You have a half a dozen nice dresses upstairs in your closet."

Savannah scrambled back to her feet, full of animation once again. "It has to be brand-new, Daddy." She spread her hands wide for emphasis, frustrated that he didn't intuit this on his own. "Everybody is getting *brand-new* dresses to wear. Everybody went shopping for their very special dress with their mommy except me." Tears filled her eyes, "And I didn't get to because I don't have a mommy!"

Talk about a dagger to the heart, Alexis thought.

Grady looked as crushed as Savannah and she felt. "Why didn't you tell me this sooner?" he asked hoarsely.

Mutely Savannah lifted her shoulders in a shrug.

"Grandma and Grandpa were here over the weekend," Grady continued mildly. "We could have done it then."

She shrugged again. "I guess I forgot—till I heard everybody talking about it at school today and then I got real, real sad. So you see, I can't do my homework if I don't have a pretty dress to wear."

"Sure you can." Alexis stepped in kindly. "And I'll sit with you in the kitchen while you do it."

Savannah was not happy about the idea. "But what about shopping?" she asked anxiously.

"We'll go this weekend," Grady promised.

"ONCE AGAIN YOU CAME to my rescue," Grady said an hour and a half later, after Savannah had been tucked in bed—at the child's insistence, by both of them. "I can't believe how easily you got her to complete her homework?"

Alexis shrugged off his comment. She didn't want to feel too comfortable here, or be this needed. It made her realize just how lonely she had been the past few years, while she was grieving the loss of her husband. She smiled at Grady, eager to get back to business. "We need to talk about where you go from here."

Grady walked into the kitchen. He plucked Savannah's insulated Princess lunch bag from the drying rack on the counter. "It's clear Savannah needs a mother more than ever, but the timing could be wrong."

Alexis's heart sank. "You want to wait?"

He got leftovers out of the fridge. "Yes."

Alexis could only hope this meant he was starting to come to his senses. Even though it meant they would have little or no reason to communicate with each other in the meantime. "For how long?"

He put chicken strips and dipping sauce in the lunch bag for school the next day. "Until after she graduates in ten days."

Alexis lounged against the counter and accessed the calendar on her BlackBerry. "So you want to pick it up again on July first?"

Grady added yogurt and a bag of precut apple slices. Tossed in a plastic spoon, a kid-size bottle of water and a napkin. "We're going to Laramie to spend the holiday with family. Maybe after Independence Day."

Alexis tensed. "You realize finding a mother for Savannah is going to take time," she warned. "Delaying the search won't help matters."

Arms folded in front of him, he lounged against the opposite counter. "Actually, I disagree." He shot her a significant look. "I think it will actually help in the long run."

"How so?"

He quirked a brow. "You see…I have a plan. But I need your help to pull it off."

"GRADY MCCABE WANTS TO *what?*" Holly Anne said first thing the next morning, when Alexis went in to talk with her.

"Suspend his search for a wife and have me spend more time with him and his daughter instead. On the clock."

Her boss never minded more billable hours on a project, as long as the client didn't. As far as Holly Anne was concerned, that was simply money in the bank. This request, however, was unusual. "He's paying you to spend time with them?" she repeated, stunned.

Alexis nodded. Her initial reaction had been much the same. "Grady thinks if I can spend more time with Savannah and him, I'll get to know them better and will have a more accurate idea of what kind of woman they need in their lives. And he'll be better able to assess how much of a hurry he needs to be in, when it comes to finding a mate."

Holly Anne continued opening up her mail. "You sure he's not just looking for another matchmaking service on the sly? Maybe thinking of going with one of our competitors?"

At the moment, Alexis honestly didn't know what to think. "I offered to set him up with another matchmaker here."

"And?" her boss pressed, putting one letter into the In basket, another in the trash.

"For whatever reason...Grady's little girl has gotten rather attached to me," Alexis stated carefully. "She's been having a hard time. That translates into a lot of chaos in his life. Which is why he wanted a wife as soon as possible. Now that he's met with three women, none of whom were right, he's not so eager to continue screening candidates and introducing them to his daughter." She exhaled. "And I can hardly blame him for that. He's busy enough as it is, with this new project he has going downtown. To put all this additional pressure on himself—and by association, Savannah—well, it seems to be making the situation worse."

Holly Anne picked up the last letter in the stack. "Will you being there, billing him by the hour, help the overall situation?"

Truth time. "It could."

"Will it lead to him looking again?"

Alexis hesitated. "Maybe." She hated to think how much she loathed the idea of seeing him with yet another marriage-hungry woman. "But I'll be honest. I still can't promise anything."

Holly Anne sat down at her desk, switched on her computer. "Why not?"

"Because even though it's been five years, I just don't think he's completely over losing his wife." Instead, he seemed to be waiting for something awful to happen again the moment he got happy, and Alexis knew how that felt. Once life had taken a truly devastating turn, you were never without that niggling bit of fear in the back of your mind.

It was hard, moving on.

Her boss knew that, too.

When she finally spoke, her tone was grave. "The other partners are excited about having someone with Grady's stature as a client. If you don't match him with anyone, or at least get him looking again, this will impact your chances of getting the Galveston job and the substantial pay raise that goes with it—no matter how many hours you bill."

Alexis nodded. "I assumed that would be the case." How many times had she been told that, in their company, *results* were what mattered?

"Don't disappoint me, Alexis," Holly Anne warned quietly. "We're counting on you to make the match of the century for Grady McCabe."

SAVANNAH'S MATH HOMEWORK looked easy enough to Alexis, when she sat down at the kitchen table with Grady's little girl early that evening. "Hmm..." She pretended to be perplexed as she studied the mimeographed sheet of eight problems. "I'm not really sure what we're supposed to do here...."

Savannah's eyes widened, as if amazed Alexis could be so dense. Glancing back at the paper, she picked up a crayon. "It's easy. We just count the pieces of fruit in each box."

Alexis pointed to a box in the middle of the page, just to shake things up. "Want to do the apples first?"

"Okay!"

"Do you know how to count them?"

"Of course!" Savannah sighed in exasperation. "One, two, three!"

"Now what do we do?" Alexis probed.

"We find the number three in the box. See? Here it is. And then..." Savannah stuck her tongue between her teeth as she wielded her crayon. "We circle it, just like this!"

"Wow. That was really good," Alexis praised. "You want to show me how to do another one?"

"Sure!"

Five minutes later, they were all done. Savannah had counted objects, located the appropriate number beneath and marked it, without a single mistake. There was no doubt she was not in the least bit academically challenged by the work assigned to her. If anything, it was all too easy...and hence, boring.

"Good job, sweetheart!" Alexis said.

"Can I have a look?" Grady strolled in. Even in a rumpled shirt and jeans, with the shadow of beard on his face, the guy looked good. What could she say? No wonder the women who came over to meet him were instantly smitten. He would be quite a catch, if he ever deigned to let himself fall in love again, that was.

"Okay, but then I have to put it in my backpack to take to school tomorrow," Savannah told her father importantly.

Gravely, Grady perused the work sheet with Savannah's

name written awkwardly across the top. "That's excellent!" he told her. "I'm very proud of you!"

Savannah beamed. Familial warmth permeated the room. Amazed that her work there could have been completed so quickly, Alexis looked at Grady, wondering what was next.

"Want to help Savannah and me make dinner?" he said.

"What are we having?" Savannah asked excitedly.

"Your favorite. Pizza. Run upstairs and change into some shorts and a T-shirt and I'll let you pat out the dough."

"Okay, Daddy!" Savannah raced off, anxious to get out of her school uniform.

Grady and Alexis exchanged glances, the air vibrating with tension.

Once again, Alexis noted, she and Grady were alone. And having all that raw male power focused on her was unsettling, to say the least.

ALEXIS WASN'T SURE what she had expected for the rest of the week. What she got was more of the same. She worked all day at the office, matching other couples with her usual exceptional success. Then arrived at Grady's shortly after Savannah got home from her after-school program, at five-fifteen. Homework was done at the kitchen table, followed by dinner, which more often than not was now a group cooking project. Then there was bath, story and bedtime, and finally a casual adieu.

Savannah was always overjoyed to see her and sad to say goodbye. Grady treated Alexis with kindness and reverence. Occasionally she found him looking at her a tad too long. But out of respect for her previously stated wishes, he always turned away.

There were no accidental touches or near kisses. No physical contact between the two of them of any kind.

His chivalry was driving her crazy. She wanted, she realized belatedly, to connect with him again. Even if it wasn't what *he* wanted.

And yet she knew he was right, keeping the relationship between them strictly platonic.

When Savannah completed the school year, Alexis still had to match him with someone else. A woman who wouldn't require love.

Which was why, Friday evening, Alexis was thinking about making an excuse to leave early, as soon as Savannah's homework was done. Before she was overcome with wistfulness for what could never be.

And that was, of course, exactly when Savannah turned her hope-filled gaze upon her. "Are you coming shopping with me and Daddy tomorrow morning?" she asked. "For my graduation dress?"

"Actually…" Grady stepped away from the fridge, where he was busy studying the contents. "I was meaning to talk to you about that."

"Daddy said you can come with us and help me try on the dresses!" Savannah said.

His eyes on hers, Grady moved closer. "She wanted a woman's point of view, and since my mom's off on an oil rig in West Texas, and can't be here until the day of graduation…"

"Say yes!" Savannah grabbed on to Alexis and held on tight.

There went her plan to have a respite from the family that was beginning to feel far too much like her own.

"Please, please, please!" Savannah looked up, waiting.

There was no way Alexis could deny the need shimmering in those sweet blue eyes. She caved. "Of course I'll come," she promised. It was little more than an errand, after all. Something she'd do for any friend with a daughter Savannah's age. And if Grady happened to be along for the trip, so be it.

He grinned, his smile so wide and all-encompassing it crinkled the corners of his eyes. "That's great," he said, looking more cheerful than he had all week. Despite her decision to keep a wall between them, Alexis found herself smiling back at him.

"Now for the bad news." Grady twisted his handsome face into a comical parody of apology. "I thought we still had some stuff in here to make tacos, but we don't, so what do you ladies say about going out for dinner tonight? It is Friday, after all."

Savannah jumped up and down in enthusiasm. "I want to go to a restaurant!" she declared.

"And then maybe stop by the grocery store on the way home?" Grady looked at Alexis. "That is, unless you've got other plans…?"

Was he fishing to find out if she had a date? The thought that he might be sent a thrill of excitement through her. Alexis forced herself to calm down. Since their one ill-advised tryst, Grady had given her no reason to think that he wanted anything more from her than help with his daughter.

Before she could stop herself, she smiled again, more casually this time, and said, "Nothing I'd rather do."

Grady grabbed his keys and BlackBerry while Savannah ran upstairs to change into a ruffled T-shirt, matching lavender shorts and sandals. The three of them walked outside. They were nearly to Grady's SUV when a sleek Jaguar sedan pulled into the driveway.

Kit Peterson was behind the wheel. She waved, turned off the engine and got out. The statuesque redhead strode toward them, her high heels clattering on the driveway.

"Hello, Grady! Savannah. And—?" She slid her sunglasses partway down her nose and peered over the rim.

"Alexis Graham," Alexis reminded her, trying not to grimace.

"Oh, right..." Kit greeted her with a dismissive nod, then turned back to Grady, an exaggerated expression of sympathy on her perfectly made up face. "I just came over to see how you all were doing!"

Wild giggling emanated from the back of the Jaguar.

Lisa Marie and two other little girls from Savannah's class were clearly visible. They were pointing and ducking down in the back seat, obviously making fun.

Alexis felt Savannah tense beside her.

She put an arm around the child, who leaned against her with a slow exhalation. Alexis sensed her unhappiness. She knew it wasn't her place, but oh, how she wanted to reprimand the trio responsible for Savannah's obvious discomfort.

"What's going on?" Grady asked Kit.

"Just a minute." the woman tottered back to the sedan. "Girls!" she scolded. To no avail—the giggling died down momentarily, before starting up again. Kit leaned into the open window, treating her audience to a view of the tight white skirt encasing her slender backside, as she retrieved a ribbon-wrapped bakery box. Nose in the air, she did her beauty queen walk back, knelt and gave it to Savannah. "Here you go, darlin'. This should make you feel all better."

Savannah held the box, from a popular cupcake emporium, as if it were radioactive.

"I have no idea what you're talking about," Grady said.

Kit looked flummoxed. "Well, I assumed," she said dramatically, "you would have chatted with Principal Jordan...."

"About?" he demanded, still in the dark.

"Oh, dear!" Kit draped a hand across her chest. "It seems I spoke too soon."

The lenses of the woman's sunglasses were opaque, so Alexis couldn't see her eyes, but was pretty sure she knew how they'd look. Mean girl, all the way...

Grady must have known it, too. And he was beginning to get really ticked off.

"You know what?" Having done the damage she clearly intended to do, Kit gave an airy little wave. "I think I'm just going to go ahead and leave. I'm taking the girls to a movie tonight and I don't want to be late. So we'll talk later. You call me if you need to, Grady dear." She smiled condescendingly at his daughter. "Savannah, good to see you, darlin'. And Alexis, do call me. I think I can help you out with some ideas for..." She smiled at Grady mysteriously. "Well, you know...."

As if, Alexis thought grimly, she would ever match Grady with one of Kit's friends!

"Thanks for the cupcakes," Grady stated politely, sounding anything but grateful.

Kit Peterson drove off, the three little girls in the back of her car still giggling unkindly.

Savannah appeared ready to cry.

Grady glanced at his watch. "You know what, ladies? I forgot I have to make a call first. So if you want to take those cupcakes inside and put them on the counter, I'll slip into my study and do that before we get on our way."

Savannah didn't say anything. Head down, still carrying the pastry box, she headed for the front door.

Grady traded glances with Alexis over his daughter's head. On this, Alexis knew without saying a word, she and Grady were in perfect agreement. They both wanted to throttle their recent visitors for hurting his little girl's feelings.

Chapter Nine

"Did you get hold of Principal Jordan?" Alexis asked.

"Finally." Grady set the tray of food on the table next to the play area in the popular fast-food restaurant. From where they were sitting, they could see Savannah, and four other children racing around the elevated tunnels, mesh-sided walkways and dual circular slides. All were well out of earshot, and clearly having a fabulous time.

Grady handed Alexis her flame-grilled burger and onion rings, and confided, "She said she didn't want to get into it over the phone. That we'd talk in her office Monday morning at nine o'clock."

Alexis tensed. "That sounds ominous."

"I asked Principal Jordan if Savannah was in some sort of trouble and she assured me that was not the case," he continued, obviously sharing Alexis's concern.

She studied Grady's worried-looking face. He didn't let his guard down very often. She knew the fact he was doing so now—with her—was significant. "You're not buying it?" she guessed in the same low tone.

Grady tore the paper wrapper off his own burger and stuck a straw in his soft drink. They had promised Savannah she wouldn't have to eat until after she had played awhile, so her meal remained on the tray.

There was a moment of warm familiarity when his gaze met Alexis's. This was what it would be like to be married to Grady and raising his daughter. This feeling that whatever problems came up, they would handle them together....

"If it wasn't bad news, why all the mystery?" Grady mused, searching her eyes.

"Why Kit Peterson's sanctimonious attitude?" Alexis countered.

"Exactly." He spread his napkin across his lap and picked up his double cheeseburger. "I hate this, having her in an all-girls school. I feel so out of my league."

Alexis imagined everyone who wasn't in the school's estrogen-driven in crowd felt that way.

"Which is why," he continued, some of the brooding intensity leaving his face as he looked at her yet again, "I was hoping you'd go with me Monday morning."

"For moral support," Alexis suggested, trying hard not to read more into it than that. "For you and Savannah."

He acknowledged it with a shrug, adding, "And you're a woman. You've worked with Savannah on her homework. You know how bright she is. And last but not least, I think you have more objectivity than I do right now."

Alexis wasn't sure about that. She was feeling pretty emotional about the way Savannah was being treated by Kit Peterson, her daughter and classmates, as well as the school administrator. None of it seemed on the up and up, but then what did she know about the rarefied world of private girls schools? "If you think I can help," she allowed, pushing away those turbulent thoughts.

Grady reached over and briefly touched her hand. And in

that moment, all the casualness of their conversation transferred into something deeper. "I do," he confirmed.

The touch of skin on skin created a ripple of sensation within her. Her pulse skittering, Alexis stared into Grady's eyes. It would be so easy to fall in love with him, she realized. And so very dangerous.

"Hi, Daddy! Hi, Alexis! We're having fun up here!" Savannah shouted from up above, her grinning face pressed against the mesh-sides of the walkway.

Just like that, Alexis noted in disappointment, the spell was broken.

Grady withdrew his hand and waved back. "Be careful!" he called.

"Okay, Daddy!" Savannah raced off, the other little girl and the three boys right behind her.

Grady looked at Alexis, happier now. Knowing she needed to get the conversation back on a safe, platonic topic, she took a long sip of her diet soda and asked casually, "Where did you go to school, when you were a kid?"

Grady relaxed even more. "Public school in Laramie, Texas. College at University of Texas in Austin. What about you?"

"I attended public school in Arlington, then the University of North Texas in Denton."

He dipped an onion ring in ketchup. "I guess we have that in common."

Alexis ate hers plain. "I guess we do."

They exchanged smiles again.

Okay, she thought, they really had to stop this. It was beginning to feel like a date. She concentrated on cutting her burger in half, reminding herself for the millionth time that all she was ever going to be was a family friend. "Where did you want to look for a graduation dress?"

Grady's dark brows drew together. "No clue. I thought you might have some ideas."

"Depends on how fancy you want to go, I guess."

"Knowing her classmates?" Grady said grimly. "We're aiming for the Little Princess level." He looked back at Savannah, who was still racing around, happy and carefree, then turned to Alexis once more. "Any ideas?"

Her mind jumped ahead to the possibilities. "We'll find her something every bit as special as the day. I promise."

ALEXIS MET THEM Saturday morning. Together, they hit all the high-end department stores. Savannah tried on dozens of dresses and modeled them for her daddy, but did not like a single one enough to purchase it. The more dresses she tried on, the more pouty she became.

The look Grady sent Alexis, over Savannah's head, said he was just as perplexed by his daughter's temperamental behavior as she was. Usually, he'd told Alexis before they started out, Savannah loved trying on pretty clothing.

"Maybe we should try a boutique," Alexis said.

"What's a boutique?" Savannah asked.

"A store where they only sell little girl's clothes." She consulted the list she had drawn up from her computer research, and they headed for the first shop on it. Located in a strip mall, the small store was bright and cheerful and had a rack of summer party dresses, perfect for the hot weather.

Alexis showed Savannah the ones in her size. They picked out half a dozen and went into the dressing room, while Grady sat outside to wait.

"Which one do you want to try on first?" Alexis asked.

The corners of Savannah's mouth turned down. She rubbed her toe along the carpeted floor.

Alexis sat down on the bench along the mirrored wall, so they would be at eye level. "What's wrong, sweetheart? Can you tell me?"

She shrugged, but didn't look up.

Was she overwhelmed? "Is it too hard for you to try to pick out a dress?"

A few tears trembled on Savannah's lashes and trickled down her cheek. "They're going to make fun of me," she said.

"Who is?" Alexis asked, even more gently, fearing she already knew.

The child sniffed. "Lisa Marie and all her friends."

Alexis reached out and drew her onto her lap. "Why would they do that?"

Savannah cuddled close and rested her head against Alexis's shoulder. "They're going to say I look stupid, 'cause I don't have a mother to help me buy a dress, and then they're all going to laugh at me."

Savannah wrapped her arms around Alexis's neck, and the damn broke. She cried silently, her whole body shaking. As she witnessed the little girl's misery, it was all Alexis could do not to break down, too. Her own eyes blurred with tears as she murmured soft reassurances.

Finally, Savannah got it all out and settled down.

Alexis stroked a hand through her curls. Still holding her tight, she pressed a kiss to the top of her head. "I am so sorry those girls hurt your feelings. That is not nice. Not nice at all."

Savannah sniffed some more. Still holding on, she leaned back enough so she could see Alexis's face. "I'm not mean to them."

Unfortunately, Alexis thought sadly, that did not always matter. "I'm glad to hear that, Savannah. Because all being mean to someone else does is make you feel bad inside."

Savannah clearly didn't quite believe that. Which was why they needed to bring Grady into the situation, to offer counsel and advice, Alexis decided. "Tell you what. I think we've had enough shopping for one morning. Why don't we forget about trying all these dresses on and go get your daddy and have lunch instead?"

Savannah's body sagged with relief. "Okay," she said with a tremulous smile. She took Alexis's hand. Together, they went to find Grady.

GRADY DIDN'T ARGUE WITH the abrupt break in the shopping excursion. In fact, he looked every bit as relieved as his daughter to be able to go to a nearby barbecue place. Exhausted, Savannah fell asleep in the car on the way home afterward. He carried her inside and upstairs to her bed. When he came back down, Alexis was waiting in the living room.

"Is she still napping?"

He nodded. "Out like a light."

Alexis was glad. "We need to talk."

"I figured." Grady sat down next to her on the sofa. Once again it felt more like they were co-parents than just friends. "What happened in the dressing room at the last place?" he asked. "When Savannah came out she looked like she had been crying."

"Yes. I wanted to speak with you about that privately before you talked to her." Briefly, Alexis filled him in.

Grady's jaw hardened at the news of what the other little girls were saying to his daughter at school, when the teacher wasn't within earshot.

"Normally, knowing there are two sides to every story, and sometimes things can be said one way and taken another, I'd suggest you investigate more," Alexis stated. "Give the kids the benefit of the doubt. But having seen Lisa Marie and her little pals in action last night, the way they seemed to be taunting Savannah from the back seat of Kit's Jaguar, I imagined Savannah's account is all too true."

Grady looked deeply concerned, and once again way out of his league. "What do we do in a situation like this?"

Alexis tried not to focus on the "we" in his sentence. It was figurative, just an expression. She shrugged. "I was going to ask you."

"That's the hell of it." He shoved his fingers through his hair, stood and began to pace. "I don't know."

Alexis stayed seated. Savannah was Grady's child—it should be his decision. "What's your first instinct?"

"To talk to the kids' parents. In this case, though, I don't think it would do any good, since children model their parents' behavior."

And Kit Peterson was snotty to the core.

Grady stared off into the distance. "If she were a boy—"

"What would you advise?"

"That he fight back. Stand up for himself."

Alexis thought about her own counsel to turn the other cheek. "What would your late wife have said?"

"She probably would have gotten into it with Kit Peterson. Called her out and had a row. Tabitha was not one to shy away from quarrels with other women. In fact, I think there was a part of her that enjoyed those cat fights."

Interesting. It was the first time Alexis had heard Grady speak about his wife with anything other than total reverence. "Of course, the real problem is that these girls are in her class at school and she can't just avoid them."

Alexis thought about the mother-daughter tea party coming

up. "Maybe you could bring this up at the meeting on Monday with the principal."

"I don't think we should involve her." He paused. "At some point, Savannah does have to learn to stand up for herself."

"Grady. She just turned five."

"So you think the fact I want to give those little girls a talking-to myself without involving Principal Jordan is not out of line?"

Alexis exhaled slowly. "Not at all." She looked up at him. "Your mom seems very capable. What would she say?"

Grady's eyes glimmered. "She always wanted us to fight our own battles, but I can remember a time or two when she stormed into a school to give someone her opinion."

Alexis rose and moved closer. "Did it help?"

"Sometimes." Grady shoved his hands in the pockets of his shorts. "Sometimes not. I always felt better knowing she was on my side, though. There's something to be said for having a parent as your staunchest defender. It makes you feel safe."

"Yes," Alexis said, remembering a time or two when her own parents had gone to bat for her. "It does."

They looked at each other, in sync once again. Grady flashed her a bemused smile and she smiled back.

"Fortunately," he said with a sigh, "kindergarten graduation is just six days away. After Thursday, she won't see those girls until the new term school starts on August first."

Not much of a break, Alexis thought. And nothing much would change to help the situation. Plus, there was the tea party at the Peterson home coming up in five days, although she figured they should hold off discussing that and just concentrate on one problem at a time.

Grady turned back to her. "What do you think we should do about the dress?"

Alexis shrugged helplessly. "I'm not sure. Savannah isn't confident she can pick anything out that's going to be bully-proof."

He leaned against the fireplace mantel with a rueful grimace. "Nice way to put it."

"I call it like I see it in instances like this," she said quietly.

Grady's eyes narrowed. "You think I should take her out of Miss Chilton's Academy, don't you?"

Yes. The sooner the better. But Alexis knew she was on dangerous terrain here—he was still a client, after all. "That's up to you, Grady. As her parent, it's your decision," she stated carefully. "I would, however, suggest that you talk to Savannah and counsel her on how you think she should deal with female bullies. Because mean girls are tough to handle, even at that age."

Grady took Alexis's hand, then, as if realizing what he was doing, released it. "You sound like you've had some experience with this."

Alexis's skin tingled from the fleeting contact. Somehow, she forced a smile, before she edged away again. She was flirting with danger, getting so personally involved with him like this.

"I was picked on a time or two, growing up."

His gaze drifted over her lazily. He, too, seemed to be struggling to hold on to the threads of the conversation. "What did you do?"

Alexis backed up even more, pretended to inspect a photo of Grady and Savannah on the bookshelf next to the fireplace. "I usually went off to hang out with the guys." She tossed him a wry look over her shoulder. "They were much easier to get along with, even when they didn't particularly like someone."

"That's true," he admitted without a grin. "When boys get in an argument with each other, they lay it all out in the open and deal with it, and it's over."

Alexis could imagine him tussling with one—or even all four—of his brothers when he was growing up. She imagined Josie and Wade had had their hands full back then.

She swallowed around the parched feeling in her throat. "So back to the dress…?" she prodded, knowing it was time to get on task once again.

He studied her as Savannah came downstairs to join them, sleepily rubbing her eyes from her nap. "I'm guessing you have an idea?" he said as he swept his daughter up into his arms.

Alexis watched Savannah lay her head on her daddy's broad shoulder. "I do."

"YOU DON'T GET TO COME in with us, Daddy," Savannah told Grady a short time later, as the three of them stood in front of a popular bridal salon in downtown Fort Worth. Looking well-rested and in a much better frame of mind after her nap, she cupped both hands around her mouth and hissed, as if it were a secret, "This place is only for *girls*."

Grady nodded as if it was news to him. "Oh," he said gravely. He turned to Alexis with mock seriousness. "How long am I supposed to get lost?"

"I think an hour should do it," she answered. "There are some bookstores and coffee shops down the block…."

Grady patted his cell phone, in the pocket of his sport shirt. "You know how to reach me. Otherwise, I'll see you ladies in an hour." He headed off.

Alexis held out her hand. Together, they went inside.

Savannah gasped in delight as she walked across the

velvety red carpet. Eyes wide, she looked at the wedding gowns displayed on the mannequins, the rows of gorgeous white dresses on hangers. "These are so fancy!"

Alexis's friend Lynn Delgado appeared. Alexis had already made prior arrangements with the bridal shop proprietress, explaining the need for TLC during this sensitive dress shopping expedition. Lynn knelt before Savannah and introduced herself. "I understand you're looking for a dress for a special occasion."

Savannah nodded vehemently. "Savannah is graduating from kindergarten on Thursday," Alexis explained.

"And I don't want to be made fun of," the child said.

Lynn, who made a living soothing nervous brides and members of the wedding party, had no problem reassuring her. "Well, I promise we will find something that is absolutely perfect for you!"

"Like a fairy princess?" Savannah suggested hopefully.

"Like the little princess you are," Lynn agreed. She led Savannah and Alexis to an area full of multicolored flower girl and bridesmaid gowns. She had already pulled out three beautifully made frocks in a classic tea-length style. "What do you think?"

Savannah shyly touched the silk chiffon with breathless reverence. "It's soft," she said.

"And very comfortable," Lynn promised. "But you should find that out for yourself. Try it on. And then come back and stand on the pedestal so you can see yourself in the three-way mirror."

Savannah glanced over at a bride-to-be doing that exact thing. Still a little awestruck, the child turned to Alexis. "But you've got to try one on, too, Alexis."

Given all it had taken to get this far, Alexis wasn't about

to rock the boat. She reached for one of the bridesmaid gowns. "Not that one!" Savannah protested. "A white one!"

Alexis flushed and knelt in front of her. "Sweetheart, those are wedding dresses."

"That's okay," she said enthusiastically, "you'll look real pretty."

"Sounds fun to me!" Lynn said.

And that, Alexis found, was that.

GRADY PACED AND BROWSED, and got a cup of coffee he didn't particularly want. Finally, forty-five minutes had passed, and he couldn't wait another moment longer. He had to know if things were going better for Savannah than they had this morning.

He pitched the paper cup in the recycling bin and headed back toward the bridal salon, figuring there'd be no harm in walking by and sneaking a look in the window.

As he reached the plate glass, a happy bride-to-be and her mother swept out of the shop, laughing and smiling, two gowns in tow.

Grady stopped to hold the door for them and then turned to shut it, noticing as he did so that his gallant action gave him a clear view all the way to the rear of the store, where three pedestals were located.

Standing on one was Savannah, in a pale yellow dress with a ribbon sash, perfect for her age. She was playing with a wreath of flowers on her head, looking happier than he had seen her in a long time.

On the pedestal next to her was an ethereal vision in white satin. The world slowed down. Nothing existed but this moment in time. He stood rooted in place as he gazed at the stunning beauty who had become such an evocative presence in their lives.

Chapter Ten

"I want you to put a wreath in your hair, too!" Savannah said, giggling.

"I already have a veil," Alexis protested, feeling a little silly—and a little magical—in the gorgeous off-the-shoulder, embroidered wedding gown.

"Pretty pretty *pretty* please!" Savannah jumped up and down on the pedestal next to hers. "I want us to match!"

"Then that's what you shall have, my little princess." Alexis stepped down off her pedestal. Savannah did the same. Closing the distance between them, Alexis gathered her train in both hands and bent down, in a deep curtsy. Grinning, Savannah stood on tiptoe, and with all the reverence of a flower girl assisting a bride, gently laid the wreath of flowers on top of Alexis's hastily upswept hair.

Finished, Savannah stepped back to admire her handiwork, then clapped her hands together. "Now you look really pretty!"

Silly was more like it, with a tiara and veil perched on the back half of her head, a wreath of flowers slanting down over her forehead. Still, Alexis couldn't help but laugh aloud. She had forgotten what it was like to let go of life's problems and difficulties and just do whatever made her happy.

She bent down and gathered Savannah into a heartfelt hug. "You look incredibly pretty, too, sweetheart."

"This is the dress I want to wear to my graduation," Savannah declared, 'because it's the color I like the mostest."

Alexis stepped back to admire her once again. "I think that's a very good choice, Savannah. You look very pretty in yellow."

"You both look very pretty," a male voice interjected.

In unison, Savannah and Alexis turned toward the sound. Grady stood there, smiling as widely as his daughter.

Alexis blushed as she hadn't since she was a gawky teenager.

"This time we tried on dresses together!" Savannah said. "And it was way more fun, Daddy."

"I can see that," he murmured, an appreciative glimmer in his eyes.

Lynn, who'd been busy with another customer, came bustling back. "How are we doing?" she asked.

Alexis confirmed the purchase with both father and daughter, then said, "We're going to take the yellow dress for Savannah."

"Are you going to get yours, too?" the child asked.

"Not this time," she answered.

Savannah's face fell. Then she perked up. "Does this mean we get to come back and try on dresses again?"

Aware of Grady's eyes upon her, Alexis blushed all the more. "Maybe the next time you need a special dress," she allowed.

TO CELEBRATE THE successful purchase of a graduation dress, they stopped by the park to let Savannah romp in the shady playground. While Alexis lounged on a bench, watching her race over climbing equipment with a group of other kids, Grady ambled off to purchase cold drinks for all of them.

He returned with three tropical slushies. Savannah ran over to take a long drink of hers, then left the icy beverage with her daddy while she returned to her new friends.

Grady dropped down beside Alexis and stretched out his legs. The look in his eyes made her flush from the inside out. "You can stop blushing now," he teased.

Alexis focused her gaze straight ahead. "You can stop looking at me as if you're still seeing me in that gown."

"Can't help it." He shrugged and glanced away. "You were gorgeous."

Alexis took a pull on the straw, enjoying the tropical fruit flavor, the crushed ice melting on her tongue. "I know I shouldn't have tried it on. I just wanted to distract Savannah, wipe out the memory of our disastrous shopping trip this morning. And I know how much she likes playing dress-up, so when she insisted I try on a gown alongside her, I said yes."

His gaze returned to hers. "You don't have to explain."

She knew that. So why was she? Why did it matter so much how Grady McCabe saw her?

His dark brows lifted slightly and one corner of his mouth turned up in that lopsided smile she found way too sexy for her own good. "I enjoyed seeing you in a wedding dress. It gave me an idea of what you must have looked like the first time around."

Not quite. "Scott and I didn't have a big wedding."

Clearly, that surprised him. And she knew why. Most self-avowed romantics like herself insisted on them. "We eloped."

"Is that what you wanted?"

Yes and no. "I really wanted to be with him," Alexis said softly.

"Why do I think there's more to this story?" he mused.

Because there was. Aware she had never talked about this

with anyone, Alexis shrugged, as if it hadn't really mattered, when she knew, deep down, that it had. "He was pushing us to move in together." And at the time, she had lacked the confidence to stand up to him. "Economically, it made sense. We were both just out of college, and neither of us could afford much on our own. Together, with both of us working, we could afford a nice two bedroom apartment and two decent cars, and to start saving for a down payment on a house. And he thought eloping was the most romantic way of all to marry."

Grady's face softened. "And you went along with it to please him. Circumventing what you really wanted—a fairy-tale wedding."

Alexis sipped her drink and looked into his eyes. "It seems Savannah and I have that in common. We both love really fancy dresses."

They fell into a thoughtful silence once more.

"Any regrets?" Grady asked, gauging her reaction.

Alexis shook her head. "I've always believed that things work out the way they should. Forgoing the big wedding gave us another year of marriage. I thought about that a lot as Scott battled leukemia."

"Next time," Grady said quietly, with understanding reflected in his deep blue eyes, "maybe you'll get what you want."

"I will," Alexis said. Or she wouldn't marry. She turned toward him, her knee nudging his thigh slightly in the process. "What about you?" she asked, shifting slightly on the bench, so they were no longer touching. "Did you and Tabitha have a formal wedding?"

Grady nodded, and waved at Savannah, who was still happily monkeying around on the climbing gym. "We married here in Fort Worth."

Alexis regarded him curiously. "Was it everything you wanted?"

"Except for the location." He shrugged. "I would have preferred having it in my hometown, but I deferred to her wishes."

Alexis appreciated his gallantry. "Seems you and I have that in common." A habit of putting others before themselves....

"As well as something else," Grady said.

She shot him a baffled look.

"When I saw you in that dress today, laughing and hugging Savannah, I realized it's not just my little girl who wants me to be married again," Grady explained. "I want that, too."

ALEXIS SWALLOWED, not sure she'd heard right. "You're serious?" she said, when at last she could speak again.

Grady nodded. He waved at Savannah, who was now sitting atop the fort-style play gym, talking to two other little girls and a boy. Although they had never met before, they seemed to be having a good time.

His expression sober, Grady continued, "It made me think how much Savannah and I have both enjoyed having you with us this last week, helping with homework and dinner and bedtime and dress shopping. I realized how much we would be shortchanging ourselves if I married someone under the guidelines I originally set up with your matchmaking service."

At last he had come to his senses! Alexis thought jubilantly, aware how much easier that would make her job, professionally speaking. Emotionally was another matter. It was going to be tough for her to watch him fall in love with someone else. Harder still to watch another woman step into the intimate day-to-day activity of Grady and Savannah's lives. And yet she knew he would be so much better off if he let himself be loved again, so she had to be happy about that.

Determined to do the right thing and help make that happen, she forced herself to be the premiere matchmaker he had hired. "So you want to change your requirements in a potential spouse? Redo your profile and questionnaires and video interview?"

"Not necessarily," he said, with that Difficult Man note in his tone again.

Her emotions awhirl, Alexis tightened her grip on the drink clutched in her hands. "Well, I guess I can just interview you about what you want in a wife, and make the adjustments myself." It wasn't the usual procedure, but then what about her relationship with Grady had been ordinary thus far?

He turned toward her and draped his arm along the back of the park bench behind her. "To tell you the truth, I'd like to bypass the process altogether and just go with what I know, what has been proven to work."

She studied him, more confused than ever.

"I'd like," Grady said, "to go with you."

OKAY, GRADY THOUGHT, that hadn't come out right. But maybe there was no correct way to say it.

As the meaning of his words sank in, Alexis's mouth dropped open. Then slammed shut.

He held up a hand before she could jump to the wrong conclusion. "Obviously, that's not going to work," he admitted. "You want someone who still has all the hearts and flowers stuff in him." The kind of guy who would give her that big wedding and enjoy every second of it.

She squirmed uncomfortably.

Afraid she would bolt, given half a chance, he reached over and laid his hand on her arm. "And I want a woman who's not going to ask me to pretend to have stars in my eyes anymore," he said practically. "Unfortunately, there's no way to fix that." He dropped his voice a notch, regretting that didn't have half her optimism where his personal life was concerned.

"And that's a shame, because we get along really well in every other way." So well that he wanted nothing more than to make love to her again—without restraint this time.

"Savannah adores you," he added, "and I can see you adore her, too."

As if unable to argue with any of that, Alexis looked away. Guilt flooded Grady when he saw the sentimental glimmer in her eyes. This was exactly why he needed to stay away from her.

He forced himself to continue. "But one good thing has come out of this."

She turned back to him, and Grady lifted his hand from her arm. "The three of us have the start of a beautiful friendship. The kind that can last a lifetime. And I want it to last a lifetime, Alexis." He wanted her to know he could always be there for her, even though as yet she'd let him do precious little for her.

For a second, she looked as if they had been dating and he had just tried to break up with her. Which was kind of funny, because it was starting to feel that way to him, too. Again, not what he intended…

Then she shook her head, moved slightly away from him and visibly pulled herself together. Which was good, because he needed things to be friendly and platonic between them. In an attempt to lighten the mood, which had gotten way too serious, he teased, "If we could just clone you…"

She flashed him a feisty smile. "Or make a few slight adjustments and clone you."

He couldn't help it—he laughed.

"But," he drawled, while Alexis made a great show of sighing, "since that is out of the question, at least for now, back to finding me a wife who will accept my limitations."

Alexis plucked her BlackBerry out of her purse. "You want to start looking right away?"

Grady thought about it. Although he had realized today he wanted to be married again, the thought of spending time with another woman besides Alexis just did not appeal. "No," he said firmly. "That's going to have to wait until after the Fourth of July Day holiday."

Alexis squared her shoulders, as if preparing to do battle. "So we're talking two weeks from now?" she inquired crisply.

Grady nodded, apprehensive that in trying to be as honest as possible with her, he had nonetheless taken a grave misstep. "At the very least."

ALEXIS WAS IN THE OFFICE Sunday afternoon, filling out her time card for the previous week, when her boss walked in. "You've been logging a lot of hours lately," she noted. "How's it going with Grady McCabe?"

Alexis rocked back in her chair. "He decided yesterday he's no longer just looking for a mommy for his little girl. He wants to be married."

"Hmm. That's good." Holly Anne pulled up a chair. "Isn't it?" she asked, studying Alexis.

Doing her best to put aside her own tumultuous emotions, she picked up a pen and rapped it on the top of her desk. "I haven't a clue."

Holly Anne ran a hand through her dark hair. "What's the problem?"

"I just..." Alexis sighed and plucked at the crease on her cotton capris. "I don't know that I can please this guy."

Her boss shrugged. "You've had difficult clients before. What's different this time?"

I think I might be falling in love with him. Once again, Alexis pushed the unwanted emotion away. She had bills to pay, a promotion to earn. She had to get a grip. "Nothing, I suppose, except… He's been so determined not to get hurt again that he hasn't dated anyone since his wife died, five years ago. If he's on the rebound, it might be impossible to find a match for him that will last."

"So if we do match Grady McCabe and it doesn't work out…" Holly Anne theorized, quickly seeing the business implications of that. Alexis had already had one socially prominent couple that she'd matched—Russ and Carolyn Bass—file for divorce this month.

"I don't want to fail," Alexis said. *For more reasons than I can count.* "I don't want to put his daughter through that. Raise her hopes that she'd finally get the mommy she wants, only to have it all fall apart in the end. I think that might be devastating for Savannah." Almost as hurtful as it had been for Alexis herself, the previous day, when Grady told her he had decided he wanted a full relationship with a woman again—just, for obvious reasons, not with her.

Alexis's boss shrugged again. "I see your point regarding his daughter, but I still think you can do it."

Nothing like a little pressure.

"When is his next match supposed to take place?"

Alexis stood and went over to her bookshelves, pretending to look for something. "He doesn't want to set anything up for two weeks."

"And in the meantime?"

She picked up a stack of client videos and returned to her desk, facing her boss again. "He still wants me spending time with him and his daughter. He thinks the better I know them, the better a match I'll eventually make for them."

"I'm not certain that's necessary," Holly Anne said. Assured everything was under control, she was already on her way out. She tossed her parting words over her shoulder. "But as long as you're billing him for your time, and he's paying, who are we to quarrel?"

Who indeed? Alexis wondered.

In the meantime, she would concentrate on her other clients, while she did her best to be pals with Grady and Savannah, but nothing more.

"THANKS FOR GOING to this meeting with me," Grady told Alexis, as they walked into the lobby of Miss Chilton's Academy Monday morning.

"Happy to do it," Alexis murmured. She didn't want to see Savannah treated unfairly any more than Grady did. And it quickly became clear, as the closed-door session began, that was exactly what the headmistress had in mind.

"Before we start—I'm curious." Principal Jordan eyed Alexis with obvious disdain. "Why did you bring your matchmaker to this meeting, Mr. McCabe?"

"Ms. Graham is also a family friend. She's been working with Savannah on her homework issues and, I'm happy to report, it's no longer the problem it was for a while. Savannah sits right down every day and does her work in five or ten minutes, and puts it in her backpack."

"I'm glad to hear she is behaving responsibly." Principal Jordan paused. "However, as you know, that is not the only difficulty we have had with your daughter this spring. She's still having quite a bit of trouble socially."

Grady's jaw set. "Are we referring to the way the other little girls are picking on her?"

Briefly taken aback by his blunt assessment of the situation, the administrator responded, "We're referring to her apparent inability to hold her own in a convivial setting. Which is why we still think it would be wise for Savannah not to graduate with her classmates on Thursday afternoon, and instead repeat her kindergarten year."

Silence fell.

"You've got to be kidding," Grady said finally.

Principal Jordan shook her head. "Quite the contrary."

"There's no way I'm going to agree to this," Grady stated, his expression grim. "She has done all the work, and earned the right to move on to first grade, along with all her friends."

Alexis admired the way he stood up for his daughter. It was exactly what she would have done.

"That's the problem," the principal admitted with obvious discomfort. "Savannah doesn't have many friends in her class. We were hoping—the other teachers and I—that it would be different next year."

"How? Can you guarantee there will be kinder, more empathetic girls in her class? Or just more of the same, tormenting her over her lack of a mother?"

The administrator leaned across her desk. "I would thank you," she said tightly, "not to refer to our students that way."

Grady stood, a muscle working in his jaw. "I paid twenty thousand dollars in tuition for Savannah to attend kindergarten at her mother's alma mater. She has attended school regularly and done the work. She will graduate with her peers and be promoted to first grade, along with everyone else in her class."

Principal Jordan stared at Grady. "Very well. Savannah will be promoted—with reservation—and can attend her graduation on Thursday, along with all her peers. But I must warn you, Mr. McCabe. Should her problems with Lisa Marie Peterson and some of the other little girls *continue* next autumn, we will revisit this issue. And if necessary, move Savannah back to kindergarten then."

So *that's* what was going on here, Alexis thought angrily. Kit Peterson was behind this! She'd had a feeling ever since Kit showed up at the house on Friday that she had something up her sleeve.

Grady took a moment to absorb the thinly veiled threat, then stated in a low, implacable tone, "It won't be an issue when the new school term starts."

Alexis believed him. She just didn't know what his next move was going to be.

She followed Grady out the door, and together they left the school and headed across the parking lot toward his SUV. Grady opened the passenger door for her. "I shouldn't have lost my temper in there," he said, starting the engine a moment later.

Alexis fastened her safety belt. "You had every right to be disgusted. I certainly was."

Grady looked at her. "Well, now we know why they brought cupcakes for Savannah Friday evening."

"And were giggling and making fun of her that way."

Stopping at a traffic light, Grady turned to Alexis. "Why would they want Savannah out so badly?"

Noting he was hurting for his daughter, as much as Alexis was, she tried to explain. "She's very pretty and smart. Maybe too nice to be in a cutthroat environment like that. Unless…"

"What?"

She had to say it. "You want her turning into a mean girl, too."

"Hell, no." Grady's jaw set as he drove on.

"Well, then, it looks like you're going to have to do something about it. Either take on Kit and her daughter's entourage and make them all behave, or move Savannah out of there and put her in another school."

They reached his driveway, where Alexis had left her car. "Do you have time to come inside for a moment?" he asked, his expression pensive.

Alexis glanced at her watch. Her first appointment with a new client was not for another hour and twenty minutes. "Sure."

"I'm going to have to find another private school for Savannah," he said, leading the way into his study and switching on his computer. "I was hoping you'd help me look for a good match. On the clock, of course."

His mention of money sent her spirits into a nosedive. Alexis had to work to keep from showing her hurt. "Of course. And here I thought I was just put on this earth to help people find love."

The sarcasm in her voice caught his attention. "Very funny." He motioned for her to have a seat at his desk. "Seriously, it's going to be difficult, at this late date, to find a spot for her this fall."

Alexis slipped into his swivel chair. It felt oddly intimate, sitting where he usually did. She lifted her face to his. "If you don't mind my asking...what's wrong with public school?" She didn't let the hesitant look on Grady's face keep her from speaking her mind. "I went there," she continued. "You went there. We both had good experiences. Why does it have to be private?"

Grady sat down on the edge of his desk, facing her. "Why indeed?" he murmured. "You're right that I should consider it. Whenever I take Savannah to the playground—or anywhere there are kids from varied backgrounds—she does great. It's only when I stick her with a bunch of little blue bloods that the atmosphere becomes intense."

Alexis rebuked him with a look. "Well, I don't think we should discount all rich kids, as a rule. I mean, you come from wealth, Grady, and you turned out pretty great."

He flashed her a sexy grin. "You think so?"

She caught the look in his eyes. Hitched in a breath at the warm intimacy beckoning her near. Aware that she was way too close to falling head over heels in love with him as it was, she reminded herself that Grady was not interested in letting anyone into his heart again, even if he did want to marry. As for her, she needed much more than a simple legal commitment from a man to say "I Do" to him.

But from the determined look in his eyes, he clearly had his mind made up.

Grady wrapped one hand around her wrist, pulled her up out of his chair, and reeled her in to his side. Caught off balance, she crashed into him, her body rubbing against his. He clamped an arm around her waist, holding her close, then reached up to tuck a strand of hair behind her ear. She trembled as he stared soulfully into her eyes. "Have I told you," he asked softly, "just how fantastic you've been the last couple of weeks?"

A ripple of need swept through her, followed swiftly by a wave of feelings she could not deny. "Grady…"

"Just one kiss, Alexis," he murmured tenderly, his lips shifting toward hers. "Just one…simple…kiss. What can that hurt?"

Chapter Eleven

What one kiss could hurt, Alexis knew, was her ability to go on being this close to Grady without losing her head and her heart. Spellbound, she closed her eyes as his mouth captured hers, and then all was lost in the taste and touch and feel of him.

He was so big and blatantly male. His kiss so incredibly tender and sweet. A sigh rippled through her. She lifted her arms to encircle his neck, burying her fingers in the thick strands of his hair. Giving back even as she took, she pressed forward, meeting him kiss for kiss.

Heat swept through her. Her knees wobbled with the effort it took to remain upright. The next thing she knew, he'd swung her up into his arms and was heading for the stairs.

She didn't have to ask where he was going.

She knew.

She didn't have to ask if this time they had what they needed.

She was certain that would be the case, even before he stopped to grab the box from his top bureau drawer.

Alexis had never been in his bedroom before. The furniture was heavy and masculine, the king-size bed large enough to accommodate both of them, no matter how they wanted to lie.

Legs quivering, she sat down on the taupe paisley sheets. Watched as Grady took off his coat, tie and shirt.

She'd seen him naked before. She already knew what a tremendous body he had. His shoulders were broad, his chest muscles defined, his pectorals covered with crisp, dark hair that arrowed down to the waistband of his trousers. He dispensed with those, too. Clad only in a pair of gray jersey boxer briefs that left very little to the imagination, he knelt in front of her, like a knight paying homage to a queen.

"Tell me this is what you want," he said.

Heaven help her.

"This is what I want," she agreed breathlessly.

He smiled and used his hands to part her knees. Her skirt slid up past her thighs. It was too hot to wear panty hose, so all that stood between her and what he wanted was a thin scrap of lace.

Smiling, he kissed his way from knee to inner thigh, then stood and guided her to her feet.

Their gazes locked.

He unbuttoned her suit jacket, drew it off her arms, laid it gently aside. Her lace-edged camisole came next. Then her skirt. He tugged her to him once again, one hand flattened across her spine, the other threaded in her hair. He tilted her head back, and their lips met in an explosion of pent-up heat and need.

Alexis heard the groan in the back of her throat as if from a distance. Felt the hardness of his muscles and crisp chest hair teasing the taut tips of her breasts. Lower still, there was a burgeoning pressure and heat. Dampness flowed between her thighs. She held on to his shoulders, on to him, unable to stop the sway of her body, the flood of need.

He kissed her with a sure sweet deliberation that reminded

her of everything that had been missing from her life, for so very long. Feeling as if she had come home at long last, she returned his kiss with everything she had. The brisk masculine fragrance of his cologne and the soapy clean scent of his skin filled her senses. She recalled how it had felt before, when they'd brought each other to climax, and couldn't help but want to experience the pleasure of it again—this time, with Grady buried deep inside her.

She whimpered as his fingertips played over her nipples, turning them to tight aching buds. And again, when he followed the path with his mouth, lips and tongue.

Still holding her against him, he dropped once again to his knees, this time taking off the single scrap of cloth that covered her. Grasping her hips, he buried his face in the softness of her body. He caressed the slope of her abdomen gently, ran a hand between her thighs. She cried out, feeling heat spreading through her in undulating waves, as he loved her. "Oh, Grady." She trembled helplessly as the obsession to be one with him grew ever stronger. "Not…yet…" Needing to give as well as receive, she pushed away and reached for the protection he'd provided. "Not without you."

He grinned.

Together, they removed his shorts and lay on his bed. Blushing, Alexis struggled with the wrapper, and oh so tenderly and carefully slid the condom on. Caressing him with her hands, she straddled his hips, then slowly lowered herself until they became one.

Grady groaned and grasped her waist, drawing her into an even deeper union. Then his fingers were trailing over her body, finding every responsive area, until need overwhelmed her and pleasure skyrocketed. She cried out, self-control evaporating, and the next thing she knew she was beneath him once again, euphoria flowing through her. His hard, hot body was draped over hers, and they were moving together in unison.

His hands slid beneath her. With a low moan, he lifted her higher still, possessing her fiercely. Surrendering willingly, she arched into him. Raw need gripped them both as they crested together, washed by wave after wave of sensation. Afterward, hearts pounding in unison, they slid slowly back down, into the most wonderful peace she had ever experienced in her life. And in that moment, Alexis knew there was no question about it. She was in love with Grady McCabe and always would be.

GRADY GENTLY disengaged their bodies and rolled to his side, bringing Alexis with him. Part of him couldn't believe that had just happened. The rest of him knew it had been inevitable from the start.

He hadn't been looking to fall in love. Still wasn't. Hadn't been looking to make love without any sort of commitment, either. He wasn't impulsive. He thought things through. Weighed consequences first, acted only once he knew what the stakes were, what the outcome would be. But this was different. When he was with Alexis, nothing mattered but the present moment. He felt connected to her in a very fundamental way.

She shifted, shuddered. He saw her studying him thoughtfully. Maybe even regretfully. Grady took a deep breath. Yes, the days ahead would be tricky, but together they could navigate them, if they worked together. "We don't have to figure out everything today," he murmured.

"You say that as if there is more to this than just...this," she replied.

He caught her arm before she could leave the bed, and forced himself to be ruthlessly honest. "There is," he said quietly. She was always in his thoughts. When he wasn't with her, he would find himself wondering just how long it would be before he saw her again. And since the first time they had ended up in bed, he had known they would find a way to be together again.

Apprehension laced her low tone. "I don't see how."

He paused, still struggling with his emotions. "Exactly why we shouldn't talk about it just yet," he said.

"Because we want such radically different things?"

Because he didn't want to misstep. He touched a hand to her hair, burying his fingers in the silky softness. "Because where there's a will there's a way, Alexis." He drew a long breath and looked deep into her eyes. "And what I want more than anything is you. Right here, right now, with me."

Confusion warred with the quiet deliberation on her face. "Grady…"

"We'll work it out eventually," he promised. They had to. She was the one—the only woman for him. The only mother for Savannah. Somehow, he would figure out a way to give Alexis everything she needed, to bring her all the way into their lives.

His mouth crooked up in an affectionate smile. But for now, there were more pressing needs. The desire heating their skin. The gentle give of her body that said she had been just as long without intimacy and fulfillment as him. Between the two of them, they had a lot of pent-up sexual energy. It was past time they put it to good use, because there was no way they were letting anything this good go.

Determined to make her see how great things could be if she would only put her reservations aside, he shifted so she was beneath him once more. Their eyes met. Her hands came up to clasp his shoulders and her breathing grew uneven. Slowly, deliberately, he lowered his mouth and fused his lips to hers. She ran her fingers through his hair, across his shoulders, down the center of his back. He felt her body soften as he began to explore her breasts. And knew that, no question, they were meant to be together.

This time, when the last shuddering spasm had passed, they clung together. Silent and content, they made no effort to sever the physical and emotional intimacy that had been missing for so long from both their lives.

ALEXIS WOKE TO THE late morning silence of Grady's house and the faraway sound of a cell phone ringing. A glance at her watch told her the time. She had slept through her eleven-thirty appointment with a new client!

She leaped from the bed, wrapped a sheet around herself and raced down the stairs. After checking the message and her cell phone, she swiftly dialed the office. Martha, the office receptionist, whispered, "Where are you? Holly Anne is furious! Zoe Borden asked for you personally and has waited almost a week for you to work her in—and not very patiently, I might add—and then you're a no-show?"

"I was unavoidably detained," Alexis said with as much coolness as she could muster, which wasn't a whole lot under the circumstances. She had never been this irresponsible in her life! Getting emotionally involved with a client, sleeping with him, and then missing an appointment! What was next in her long litany of mistakes? Aware that Grady had come up behind her, clad only in his boxer briefs, Alexis turned away so she could continue to concentrate on her conversation, instead of how great he looked. "Were you able to reschedule?"

"Are you kidding?" Martha yelped. "I thought she was going to blow a gasket!"

Alexis could imagine it hadn't been pleasant. Zoe Borden

was Kit Peterson's friend—the one who had wanted to be fixed up with Grady. Alexis had tried to avoid taking her on as a client, to no avail. Zoe was very wealthy and accustomed to getting what she wanted, when she wanted it. Because the customer was always right at ForeverLove.com, her wishes had prevailed.

"Holly Anne is meeting with her now. You better get here as soon as possible."

"I will. Thanks, Martha."

Alexis ended the call. Clasping the sheet around her with one arm, lifting the hem with both hands, she headed back for the stairs.

Grady followed, looking disappointed that their interlude was coming swiftly to an end. "Problem?"

"You could say that." Briefly, Alexis explained, as she rushed into the bedroom and began gathering up her clothes. What a mess. A glance in the mirror confirmed her worst suspicions: she looked like she'd spent the morning making love. Her hair was tousled, her lipstick all kissed off. Her skin radiating a postcoital glow. Holly Anne would take one look at her and know this delay had not been strictly business.

"How can I help?" he asked.

Alexis grimaced. "You can't."

They exchanged another tension-filled glance, then he went downstairs to check his own messages. Alexis finished dressing, and slipped out while he was still on the phone.

She had no choice but to stop by her apartment for a quick shower on the way to the office. When she arrived, Zoe Borden was still in with Holly Anne.

Alexis gathered her resolve, knocked, and strode on in.

Holly Anne made the introductions, adding compassionately, "Zoe has just weathered her second divorce."

And had responded, Alexis observed, by having a little "freshening" done, with mixed results. The woman's face still had the telltale puffiness and immovable quality commensurate with recent Botox. Her perfectly taut body appeared to have been enhanced by a tummy tuck and breast lift. Who knew what it looked like beneath her clothes?

Showing no evidence of the irritation Alexis knew her boss must feel, Holly Anne continued, "She'd heard that Grady McCabe was looking for a wife."

Zoe radiated cougarlike determination. "I'd like to be matched with him," she stated firmly.

"I've explained that's not how it works," Holly Anne interjected.

"But I already know Grady McCabe is exactly what I want in a man!" Zoe said petulantly.

Me, too, Alexis thought ruefully. With the exception of one tiny roadblock. As far as she could tell, Grady was still not ready to fall in love.

"There's no point in matching me with anyone else!" Zoe continued, sounding ever more agitated.

"First of all," Alexis soothed, with the most comforting smile she could conjure up, "you haven't seen any of the other candidates we might be able to match you with. We have dozens of eligible, successful, wealthy men in our database who are also looking for love, companionship and someone to build a future with. You would be limiting yourself terribly if you don't allow us to show you who all is out there, before you make up your mind."

As Alexis suspected, the ka-ching of the cash register resonated with this particular client. "Well…" Zoe hesitated. "I suppose…"

Alexis slipped into the mode that had made her one of the

best matchmakers of the company. For every money-minded client like Zoe, there was a money-minded man. "Let me take you to my office and we'll get you set up with the personality questionnaires and wish lists, so we can figure out together who your dream man might be...."

An hour later, Zoe left the building with high hopes and a much more open mind. Directly after that, Holly Anne walked into Alexis's office and shut the door behind her.

Time for the mud to hit the fan.

"I think I deserve an explanation," she announced grimly

Alexis flushed guiltily. "I'm sorry." She hesitated, not sure where to begin.

Holly Anne's eyes narrowed. "I assume your absence this morning had to do with Grady McCabe?"

"He's proved to be a very demanding client," she said finally. "So demanding, in fact, that you and I need to talk."

"WHAT'S THE MATTER, pumpkin?" Grady asked Savannah when he picked her up from her after-school program that afternoon. He knew it couldn't be homework. The last take-home assignment had been given the previous Friday.

His daughter slumped dispiritedly in her seat. "Everybody else has *two* dresses. One for the graduation, and the other for the tea party at Lisa Marie's house. I only have *one.*"

Uh-oh, Grady thought. *Crisis.* "So what should we do?" he asked calmly. "Go shopping again?"

A glance in the rearview mirror showed his suggestion had gone over well.

Savannah sat up straight, smiling now. "Can we go with Alexis?"

Good question. He had left messages on Alexis's cell, home and office voice mail, but she had yet to return his calls. He hadn't spoken to her since she had slipped out of his house this morning. Not about to make a promise he couldn't keep, he said, "I think she's working late tonight. I could take you, though."

His offer was followed by silence.

Grady hazarded another glance in the mirror. Savannah's eyes met his and she gave him a soulful look, the one that always came up when the topic of her not having a mommy came up. She sighed.

"Been there, done that, hmm?" Grady mused, when they stopped at a traffic light. Another glance showed tears trembling on his daughter's lashes.

As soon as he could, Grady pulled the car over into a parking lot and put the engine in Park. He unfastened his seat belt and turned around to face his daughter. "Is anything else wrong?" he asked gently. Had Savannah heard about his private meeting with Principal Jordan that morning? Had someone told her there was pressure to hold her back a grade? If so, he thought grimly, there would be hell to pay.

Savannah turned an accusing glance his way. "Everybody else has been drinking tea and eating little sandwiches, too. And *practicing,* Daddy."

It took a moment to decipher that. "You mean they've been going to tea?"

Savannah nodded vigorously. "At a hotel."

Talk about keeping up with the Joneses! This was getting ridiculous, he thought, a little disgruntled. On the other hand, he did not want to withhold anything he could easily provide his little girl when her self-esteem and self-confidence were already shaky.

Fortunately, Grady thought, he'd have her out of this quagmire of snobbery and bad behavior soon, but until then he had a job to do. "Let me make a call. I'll see if I can figure out a good place to go."

Grady punched in a number on his speed dial. Once again, he got the voice mail for Alexis's cell. He dialed her office. Martha, the receptionist, picked up. "Grady McCabe, calling for Alexis Graham."

"Oh, hello, Mr. McCabe! Alexis said you might call. She's in a meeting. She wanted to let you know she won't be stopping by this evening. She left a message to that effect on your home phone."

She'd known he'd been at the office.

Not sure how to decipher that, Grady figured he'd find out later. He thanked Martha and cut the connection. "Looks like we're on our own tonight, pumpkin."

Grady wasn't surprised to discover Savannah wasn't any happier about that than he was.

AS THE HOURS WORE ON, Alexis's Monday went from bad to worse. She was assigned three new clients, all of them difficult personalities. The temperature in Fort Worth topped one hundred ten degrees, and the window unit in her apartment, which had been acting a little off lately, took that moment to decide to blow out nothing but hot air.

She was standing in front of it in a cotton skirt and lace-edged camisole, trying to decide if it was broken or just unable to handle the extreme heat, when a knock sounded on her door.

Already exhausted and stressed out, she walked over, peered through the viewer and saw Grady standing in the hall. He looked really ticked off. She opened the door. "Grady?"

"Just when?" he growled, shouldering past her, "were you going to tell me?"

Chapter Twelve

"Tell you what?" Alexis asked, ushering him inside.

Grady looked around, as if noticing the stifling heat inside her apartment, but didn't comment on it. He turned his intent blue eyes to hers and clarified, "That you asked your boss to assign another matchmaker to me!"

Doing her best to quell her racing pulse, she moved around him to shut the door. "You spoke to Holly Anne?"

"She telephoned me this evening." Grady's voice was calm. His emotions clearly were not. "She wanted to be sure I was okay with it."

Alexis wished she could do something about the moisture gathering between her breasts. It was beginning to seep through her camisole. And worse, Grady had noticed.

She edged toward the stream of air blowing out of her air conditioner and stood with her back to it, figuring a hot breeze was better than no breeze. Discreetly, she plucked at the fabric of her camisole, pulling it away from her moist tummy. "And were you?"

"Actually, no." Looking uncomfortably warm in his stone-colored dress slacks and starched, pale blue shirt, even though the top button was undone and the sleeves rolled up to his elbows, Grady moved toward the unit, too. "I told her I didn't want to work with anyone but you."

Alexis shifted so Grady could stand in front of what circulating air there was.

"And Holly Anne told you it was out of the question," she guessed, wishing her boss had given her a heads-up, so she would have been prepared for this confrontation tonight. She had hoped to put it off until she figured out what to say—and when to say it—knowing all the while there would never be a good time to tell Grady she was ditching him as a client.

"She said you felt someone else would do a better job." Displeasure filled his voice. "Why didn't you tell me you were going to do that?"

Alexis shrugged, and tried not to think about kissing him. "Because I thought you might try to talk me out of it."

Perspiration beaded on his face. "You would have been right."

Alexis felt her own skin dampening, too. She stepped closer, trying to adopt a practical tone as she said, "Grady, surely you can see, after what happened this morning, that I'm the wrong person to be trying to set you up with someone else."

He regarded her with the steady resolve she'd come to expect. "I don't want to be with anyone else."

A thrill shot through her at his matter-of-fact determination. "Only because you got involved with me," she countered, with the same resolve he was showing. "It still doesn't solve your problem—the lack of a mother in Savannah's life." *Or a woman you can love with all your heart and soul—in yours.*

Grady took her in his arms. "I've come to the conclusion, as has my daughter, that she doesn't need just any woman. She needs you. And so," he murmured fervently, "do I."

Before Alexis could answer, his lips captured hers. Everything she had been trying so hard to forget was suddenly at the center of her world. No one had ever kissed her as tenderly as he did, as if he cherished everything about her and wanted to experience even more. No one had ever brought forth such a wellspring of need, passion, and yes, love. When Grady pressed her against him, and made her feel as if the two of them were a perfect fit, it was all she could do to control the raging lust and soul deep yearning that blazed inside her. She wanted to be part of his life. His future. His present. She wanted to take what they had and use it as a foundation to build a love that would endure forever. She wanted to be singed by the hard muscles of his body, and filled with the most intimate part of him.

But making love with him meant being vulnerable. And she wasn't sure it was wise to feel that way tonight….

Shakily, they drew apart.

Alexis splayed her hands across his chest, forcing some distance between them. "This is what always gets us into trouble."

Grady lovingly stroked a hand through her hair. If he had any misgivings, he was not showing them, she noted.

He rubbed his thumb across her damp lower lip. "I like this kind of trouble."

So did she, on some level.

On another, more practical one, she knew she had to retain some perspective. Otherwise heartache lay ahead, and it wouldn't be just her heart that would be broken. Savannah could end up devastated, too, and what hurt Grady's child hurt him.

Still struggling to regain her composure, Alexis went to the refrigerator and got out a pitcher of water flavored with fresh mint leaves.

Grady studied her as she put ice into two glasses and then filled them to the rim. He seemed to know intuitively there was another reason why she hadn't contacted him. "What aren't you telling me?" he asked after a moment, accepting the beverage she handed him. "What else was said between you and Holly Anne?"

Alexis sat down at the café table, relieved to be able to talk about work. "A lot, actually. She's right to be very disappointed in me. You're a big client, with a lot of money and the McCabe name, not to mention being one of the movers and shakers in this city. She expected me to make a match for you that would dazzle everyone and make you very happy."

Taking a seat opposite her, Grady favored her with a lopsided grin. "Who says you haven't?"

She refused to let him distract her; he had done that far too often as it was. "I should have been focused on my job." *Instead of how attracted I am to you.* Pressing the cold glass against her forehead, to bring down the heat, she continued her litany of regrets. "I forgot what my goal as your matchmaker was, and got personally involved with you and your daughter. I ended up billing for time spent helping Savannah with her homework!"

"At my request," Grady argued, shifting his big frame in the small chair. "To help you get to know Savannah, so you would know what kind of woman she needed in her life."

It didn't matter that she had gotten her boss's approval prior to caving to Grady's request. Alexis had known on a gut level it was the wrong thing to do, professionally, but she had acquiesced because she'd wanted to spend time with Grady and Savannah. Because being with them made her feel like part of a family again. And she had needed that more than she wanted to admit—to the point she knew her judgment was hopelessly skewed, in his favor. For both their sakes, she needed to reassert her boundaries. She took a long sip of her mint-flavored ice water. Was it roasting in here or what? "Grady, I'm not a tutor."

"I agree." He drained his glass and went back to the fridge to retrieve the water. Returning, he poured them each another glass, put the pitcher on the table and sat down again. "You're more in the class of miracle worker, where Savannah is concerned. Do you know how happy you've made her and me, just being with us and resolving problems?"

As happy as it made me, taking on the mommy role? Alexis thought pensively. She sat back and rubbed at the tense spot in her neck. "But I'm not her mother, Grady. I never volunteered to be."

He studied her quietly, looking every bit as hot and uncomfortable as she felt.

"I'm not your girlfriend. I'm barely a family friend."

Grady continued to gaze at her in silence. She had the impression he wanted to argue with her about all of that. Instead, he inquired, "What does all this have to do with your job?"

Alexis let her hand drop back to her lap. "In failing you and Savannah I severely damaged my chances to run the Galveston office."

There went the promotion, the pay raise that would have quickly paid off her medical debts, the move that would have helped her start a new life. A new beginning without the reminders of the husband she had lost, and the temptation of Grady and Savannah nearby. Because as much as she loved them—and she did, Alexis realized—Grady did not love her the way he should love a woman he intended to make his wife. And she could not pretend that didn't matter to her. It did. She just wasn't sure it was enough of a deterrent to keep her from seeing Grady and Savannah again.

Had she been wrong all this time? Was getting everything she wanted from her personal life—*except* romantic love—better than being alone?

Alexis's mind told her no. Her heart felt otherwise whenever she spent time with Grady.

He reached across the table and took her hand. "You shouldn't be held accountable for my actions."

Alexis tried not to notice how good her palm felt wrapped in his. She swallowed and forced herself to look him in the eye. "My boss has every right to be unhappy with me at present. I should have been focused on business when I was working with you. I should have looked at the big picture for the Fort Worth office and thought about what my success with you could mean in jump-starting the Galveston operation. Instead..." Alexis sighed. "I lost sight of all of that, Grady, to the point Holly Anne now questions how much I want to relocate."

"How much *do* you want to relocate?" Grady asked.

That, Alexis thought, was the million dollar question. For both their sakes she forced herself to tell him what was in her heart. "I don't know." Briefly, she looked down at their hands, luxuriating in the warmth and strength of his grip. "I thought it would be a fresh start for me. A way to move ahead and put the past behind me. Now, it almost seems like I'd be running away."

From something I never should have allowed myself to get so tangled up in.

She shrugged, withdrew her hand and sat back in her chair. "I'm not sure I want to do that." Restless, she stood and walked back over to the air-conditioning unit, which was now blowing out a lot less hot air than before, although the control was still set on high.

Grady ambled after her. "I know what you mean. I've been having a few doubts myself lately."

At the mention of the word *doubts,* Alexis felt herself tense. She swung back around. "In what way?"

"This process of finding someone through a third party isn't right for me." His expression sobered. "I think part of me knew that going in—I just didn't want to admit it."

Alexis didn't know whether to feel elated or worried. "Then why did you sign up with ForeverLove.com?" she asked, before she could stop herself.

"Because Savannah needed a mommy. Still does," Grady told her seriously. "And I didn't want to go through the ups and downs of dating and all that to find her one, when I had no expectation of falling in love."

His words felt like a jab to her heart. Alexis struggled to be as professional as she should have been all along. "If I had found the right woman for you to date, I could have changed all that," she said as her AC unit made a weird crunching noise.

Grady's lips twisted ruefully. He looked past her to the poorly functioning cooling agent. "I'm not so sure. In any case," he added pragmatically, "it wasn't your fault we struck out on that score—I was an uncooperative client."

Wasn't that the understatement of the decade! Alexis began to pace, afraid if she stood next to him for much longer they would end up kissing again. "Plenty of clients are uncooperative, Grady." She went over to her hanging clothes rack, in search of cooler clothing. "In fact, when it comes to finding love via a matchmaker, I'd say that's pretty much the norm."

He watched her sort through the racks of casual clothing. "It doesn't matter. Like I said, you shouldn't be penalized for my indecision. If you want that job and the promotion that goes with it, I'll move heaven and earth to get it for you."

Alexis whirled around, not sure whether to be horrified by the possibility or amused by his offer of assistance. "You would, wouldn't you?" she observed wryly.

"All that and more," he promised. "I owe you, Alexis. For bringing me back to life."

Another ripple of longing swept through her. Alexis took another step back, banging into a row of shirts on hangers. "I don't want you to owe me."

He closed the distance between them in three long, lazy strides.

"I don't want us to be on the clock." She gulped as he ran his hands up and down her bare arms. She trembled, asserting, "If we ever make love again—"

"We will," he said emphatically, as sure about that as she secretly was.

"I want it to be..." Alexis searched for the right words "...without complications. I don't want to worry about the ethics of it, or the long- or short-term implications, Grady. I just want to live in the moment, appreciate what we have while we have it."

At least for now, until she figured out whether or not she was going to be content with the limitations he'd set over the long haul. "Can we do that?"

"We can do anything you want." Grady pulled her into his arms and delivered another searing kiss. "But there's one thing I want *you* to know, Alexis. I told your boss I'm out, no longer a client of your company. I already know what I want... and it's not that."

GRADY EXPECTED ALEXIS to be happy about that. Instead, she looked upset. "How did Holly Anne take it?" she demanded.

He shrugged. "About how you'd expect. She tried to talk me out of it. When that didn't work, she wanted to know if you were to blame. I assured her that was not the case. You had gone far above and beyond your responsibilities as my matchmaker to try and pair me up with someone, under the very trying parameters I had set." He sighed. "To no avail. Savannah wasn't happy. I wasn't, either. I was trying to hire a mommy slash wife the same way I'd hired a nanny—and it just wasn't a workable situation."

"I'm glad you realize that." Alexis's eyes softened. "Because I think you and Savannah deserve a whole lot better than that, too."

Grady nodded in agreement. "In any case, I promised Holly Anne if I decided to go that route again, I would use ForeverLove.com. And to make up for the way I've monopolized your time, and distracted you to the point you missed a client meeting this morning, that I would give a testimonial the company could use in their advertising."

"That must have pleased her!"

To put it mildly. "I did my best to turn a negative into a positive for you."

"Thank you."

Grady walked over to see what he could do with the AC—it was hotter than blazes in here! "So when will you find out if you get the Galveston job or not?" he asked, over his shoulder.

"Thursday." She followed.

"The day of Savannah's graduation." He studied the controls. Nothing seemed amiss.

"Speaking of the little darling, where is Savannah?"

Grady smiled fondly. "With a sitter. I tucked her in before I left. She was so tired, she was asleep before the lights were out."

"Poor kid."

He noted the perspiration dampening Alexis's clothes—and his. "What's wrong with your air conditioner?"

"It doesn't seem to be working. I called building maintenance, but I doubt I'll hear back from them until morning."

"Well, you can't stay here. People die in this kind of heat. It must be a hundred degrees in here."

Alexis lifted the hair off the back of her neck. "I was just thinking about going to a hotel."

Grady had already cost Alexis enough. This was one expense he could easily alleviate. And since he already knew she wouldn't let him pay...

He took her by the hand, anxious to get her someplace cool and comfortable. "You're coming home with me."

ALEXIS WOKE TO THE JOYFUL sound of Savannah's voice. "Daddy! Daddy! Alexis is here! She sleeped in one of our beds!"

Footsteps sounded outside the guest room door. "Slept," Grady corrected. "And shhh! We don't want to wake her."

"I'm up." Alexis opened her eyes.

Savannah dragged Grady all the way into the room. "Hi, Alexis!" She dropped his hand and climbed up on the bed. "What are you doing here?"

Alexis stifled a yawn and struggled to sit up. Unlike her own place, Grady's house was blissfully cool and comfortable. "The air conditioner in my apartment is broken, so your daddy invited me to sleep here last night."

Savannah cocked her head. "Your hair is pretty when it's all messy like that."

Grady seemed to think so, too. "I'll get you some coffee," he said with a grin.

Savannah sat cross-legged on the bed. "Grandma Josie is sending me a new dress for the tea party at Lisa Marie's house tomorrow."

Grady came back in with a mug, the coffee fixed just the way she liked it, with milk and a little sugar. "We talked to Mom on the phone last night." He sat on the edge of the mattress and briefly outlined the crisis that had ensued. "My mother was a Dallas debutante years ago. She has a few friends who are still in that social scene. And one of them knows an up-and-coming children's clothing designer who's going to messenger something Laura Ashley-ish over, whatever that means."

"It's going to be pretty and pink!" Savannah clapped her hands. "So now I get to wear a *pink* dress tomorrow when I go to the tea party and the *yellow* dress on Thursday when I graduate!" She held up a pair of fingers. "That's two days and two dresses!"

Alexis patted Savannah's messy curls. "Yes, it is."

The child's eyes lit up. "Can you sleep here every night?"

Alexis ignored Grady's assessing gaze as she took a sip, then set her coffee mug on the bedside table. "Um…no. Thank you for asking, though. But I'm going to have to go home when they get my air conditioner fixed."

"Is it going to be fixed today?"

"I'm not sure."

"She can stay with us until it is," Grady interjected.

"Can she go to the tea party with us tonight?" Savannah asked, slipping beneath the covers and snuggling close to Alexis. "At the hotel?"

Alexis looked at Grady. "Apparently, everyone is practicing tea party etiquette," he explained. "So we're having tea at the Adolphus Hotel this afternoon at five-thirty. Savannah and I would like it very much if you would join us."

That sounded like fun. "I would love to come," she said.

Savannah leaped up, gave Alexis a big hug and then raced off.

"Is it like this every morning?" Alexis asked.

Grady nodded. "Afraid so." He winked. "Better get used to it."

She wanted nothing more than to do just that.

TEA IN THE Lobby Living Room at the Adolphus Hotel in Fort Worth was lovely. Grady had on a jacket and tie, Alexis wore a summer business suit and Savannah looked adorable in a smocked mint-green cotton dress with short sleeves and a round, embroidered collar.

The waiters were very attentive, bringing back plate after plate of delicate sandwiches and cakes, and even serving Savannah cups of milk flavored with a bit of mild, decaffeinated tea and cubes of sugar. It was all so grown-up and 'fancy' that the little girl was beside herself.

Watching her partake of the repast, Grady couldn't stop smiling. Nor could Alexis.

Finally, they'd eaten their fill, and were waiting for the check. Relaxing in his chair, Grady told his daughter, "Now you know what to expect tomorrow when I take you to the tea party at the Petersons."

Savannah had been lounging in the curve of her daddy's arm. She sat bolt upright, utterly horrified. "Daddy, you can't go! Only mommies and little girls can go to that!"

Grady patted her on the arm. "Pumpkin, it's going to be okay. I've already RSVP'd Lisa Marie's mommy that I would be taking you, and she was perfectly fine with it."

Savannah wasn't. "But I don't want you to go, Daddy! I want Alexis!"

"SORRY TO PUT YOU on the spot like that," Grady told Alexis several hours later, when Savannah was in bed.

Alexis couldn't say she wanted to spend time at the Peterson home, but when it came to protecting Savannah from further hurt and humiliation it was a no-brainer. "I'm happy to fill in for you. Especially if it will make the event less awkward for her."

Grady took a load of clothes out of the dryer. "I'm tempted to have her skip the party entirely, but with everyone else in her class going…"

They both knew how long Savannah had been anticipating this end-of-year event. "I'll keep an eye out for her," Alexis promised, lending a hand by folding towels.

She wasn't sure whether to be grateful for or to lament the ongoing problem with her apartment air conditioning. Because the unit needed to be replaced with a new one, her place wouldn't be livable again until Friday. It seemed, with the current heat wave broiling the Fort Worth area, a lot of people were having trouble with their systems. Grady's, however, was working just fine. The heat she felt welling up inside her had everything to do with his nearness, and nothing to do with the room's temperature. "So…" she swallowed, trying not to think how much she would like to throw caution to the wind and make love with him again. "How is the search for a new school going?"

Grady went back to transfer clothes from the washer to the dryer. "I'm putting her in our neighborhood public elementary school. I spoke to the principal earlier today. It's not going to be year-round, but there's an after-school program run by the local YWCA. It includes tutoring if they need it, as well as a time for the kids to do their homework, so that's all good."

He won't need someone like me in his life.

Alexis followed Grady out into the kitchen. He opened the refrigerator and pulled out a box of pizza leftover from the evening before. The restaurant tea that had filled her and Savannah up hadn't put a dent in his hunger. Alexis shook her head, declining his offer for a wedge of pizza. "When does school start?"

Grady put two slices on a baking sheet and slid them into the oven to warm. "Last week of August." He paused to set the temperature, then went back to the fridge and got a bottle of water. "Which means she's going to have seven weeks off. And that could be a problem, as my investigation of summer day camps shows a lot of them started when the public schools let out in May, and are already full."

"Do you want me to help you with that?" The words were out before Alexis could prevent them. He was no longer her client. She was no longer billing him by the hour. But she couldn't seem to extricate herself emotionally from their problems.

Grady shook his head. "I've got it covered," he said.

A phone call from work, and some sort of emergency on the development project he was helming, occupied Grady for the rest of the evening, and was still commandeering his time and attention the next morning. So Alexis took Savannah to school, with a promise to meet her at the house in time to help her get dressed and take her to the tea party.

"Okay!" the little girl said happily, as Alexis came around to help her with her car door. "Bye, Alexis!" She awkwardly unbuckled her seat belt. Backpack banging against her leg, she tumbled out of the rear passenger seat and gave her a big hug. "See you later!" She skipped off.

Thinking maybe she had been overreacting where Savannah's previous anxiety was concerned, Alexis waved goodbye, then got back in the car and drove on to work. Maybe this tea party wouldn't be so bad, after all.

Wishful thinking, as it turned out. Savannah was tense and upset again when Alexis arrived to help her get ready. She looked adorable in the stylish new pink dress her grandmother had sent her. But shoes were turning out to be a problem. Savannah didn't like her white patent leather Mary Janes.

Grady vetoed flip-flops. "I may not know much, but I know those aren't appropriate."

Savannah scowled.

"Try again," he said.

She flounced off.

"I haven't seen her that temperamental in a couple weeks," Alexis commented.

"I know," Grady murmured, turning to her with concern. "I think it's the stress of the party. She's usually a lot better when you're around, though."

Savannah tromped back along the hall and down the stairs. She had on one red Velcro-fastened sneaker and a hot-pink rain boot. Both were for the left foot. "How's this?" she asked, in full diva mode.

Grady returned her look, his expression droll. "How do you think?"

Savannah tried to keep up the attitude, but the mixture of humor and indulgence in her daddy's eyes soon had her collapsing in giggles. Grady caught her up in his arms and hoisted her until the two were at eye level. "You know," he told his daughter, suddenly serious, "you don't have to go to this party if you don't want to."

She wriggled out of his arms.

"No." She threw herself at Alexis and held on tight. "I want to go. And I want *Alexis* to take me."

And that, Alexis thought, as she helped Grady find appropriate footwear for his daughter, was that.

FORTUNATELY, the mother-daughter tea party was in full swing by the time Alexis and Savannah arrived at the Peterson home. The unseasonably hot weather had forced the party to be held inside, instead of in the garden. White folding chairs and pastel linen covered tables for seventy dominated the formal living and dining rooms and foyer of the elegant home. Seats were indicated by place cards. A white-jacketed catering staff moved among the tables, setting up tea service and treating the little girls and their mommies to delicate pastries and sandwiches.

Savannah was right to bring her instead of Grady, Alexis thought, as the two of them found their way to their seats—at what was clearly the least desirable table, in a far corner. Already there were two other little girls from Savannah's class. Both were happy to see her. Alexis had a nice time chatting with their mothers.

Lisa Marie and the two girls who had gone out of their way to humiliate Savannah the previous week were seated at the table of honor. To Alexis's relief, they were too busy lording over their party to give Savannah any trouble.

Near the end of the event, some of the children dashed upstairs to hang out in Lisa Marie's room. Savannah stayed where she was with her friends.

And that was when one of the other mothers appeared at their table, introduced herself as Nancy Waterman, and asked to speak to Alexis privately for a moment.

Because it was convenient, they stepped out onto the screened back porch. "I'm in charge of the fittings for the school uniforms. The deadline for getting the measurements for the new first graders was yesterday at five o'clock. I've been trying to get ahold of Grady since last week. I've left messages for him everywhere, and he hasn't returned any of my calls. I thought, since you brought Savannah today, that you might know what's going on."

Before Alexis could respond, Kit Peterson popped out to join them. "Nancy…Alexis, something I should know about?" she asked brightly.

Nancy looked at Alexis, still waiting.

"Grady didn't mention anything about next year's uniforms to me," she said, quite truthfully. "But I can certainly mention it to him when I take Savannah home."

"Would you?" Nancy sighed. "This order has got to go in by Friday, and with graduation tomorrow—and the Fourth of July holiday after that—I am worried it won't get done."

"I'll talk to him. I promise," Alexis said.

"Thank you." Nancy started to go back inside.

Alexis moved to follow.

Kit stepped slightly to the left, barring her path. "We'll be there in a minute," she told Nancy with a smile. "I need to speak to Alexis, too."

The woman nodded and shut the door behind her.

"Just what is your interest in Grady McCabe?" Kit demanded.

Alexis blinked, stunned by the venom in her tone. "Excuse me?"

"You were supposed to be Grady's matchmaker, but would you ever call me back and let me help you with that? No. So I sent my very good friend—Zoe Borden—who is perfect for him, by the way—to ForeverLove.com so you could set them up." Kit's eyes flashed. "Instead, you talk her out of pursuing him! I talk her right back into it, only to find out Grady is no longer looking! And you're now cozily ensconced with him and his daughter!"

"Look." Alexis held on to her temper with effort. "I don't know what you've heard—"

"Savannah told everyone at school today you're sleeping over."

"In the guest room!" Alexis corrected, embarrassed.

Kit crossed her arms. "Mmm-hmm."

Alexis ignored the judgment in her tone. "My air-conditioning unit is broken. There's a heat wave going on, in case you didn't notice."

Kit leaned closer. "Yes, well, it's about to get a whole lot hotter if you think you're going to lay claim to that man, when there are any number of fine, socially suitable women who have been waiting for him to become available again."

When had this become a competition? Never mind one for Grady's heart? "I assure you," Alexis stated, "it was never my intention to jump line." *Never my intention to get emotionally involved with a client. Never my intention to fall in love....*

But she had fallen in love with Grady. Head over heels in love.

"That's good to know." Kit shot daggers at her. "Because all you are to him—all you will ever be—is Grady McCabe's rebound woman." Her voice dropped to a vicious hiss. "And once he's really ready to move on, you mark my words, honey. He'll come to his senses. And he'll pick someone in his own league."

Chapter Thirteen

Grady was waiting for them when they returned from the Petersons' tea. He hoisted his daughter in his arms the moment they walked through the door. "So how did it go?" he asked them, turning his McCabe blue eyes on Alexis. His probing gaze was full of something Alexis couldn't quite put a name to, but mesmerized her nevertheless.

Oblivious to the subtle sparks arcing between the two adults, Savannah snuggled closer, rested her cheek on his broad shoulder and yawned. "It was kind of boring, Daddy. We just sat at tables and ate stuff, and they didn't even have tea for the kids, like at the hotel, only lemonade with some stuff in it."

"Peach slices and maraschino cherries," Alexis interjected, in response to his baffled look.

Savannah yawned again. "I liked the tea party you and me and Alexis went to better."

"Well, I'm glad you were able to go to both," Grady said, with a perfectly solemn face, planting a kiss on his daughter's head. He cuddled her even closer. "Did you thank Mrs. Peterson and Lisa Marie for having you at their party?"

Savannah's expression indicated that was a silly question. "Of course, Daddy." She rubbed her eyes.

"What do you say we take you upstairs and get you in your pajamas and tucked in bed?" Grady smiled down at her tenderly. "You've got a big day tomorrow. You're graduating from kindergarten."

"I want Alexis to come up, too. So she can read me a story and kiss me goodnight." Savannah reached out to tug her closer.

Happy to be included, Alexis winked. "No problem."

Savannah made it through only four pages of the Dr. Seuss book she'd picked out before falling fast asleep. Her heart swelling with love, Alexis tucked the covers around her and kissed her gently, as did Grady. They both tiptoed out of the room and went back downstairs.

"So how was the party—really?" he asked as the two of them settled on the living room sofa.

Good and bad. "The catering company did a very nice job."

He admonished her with a look. "That's not what I'm asking."

She knew that. She had just been hoping to avoid discussing anything that would spoil the peaceful, relaxed mood. Alexis focused on the concern in Grady's gaze. "All the girls were on their best behavior. And it helped that Savannah and I were seated a great distance away from Lisa Marie and her friends." Alexis did her very best to be objective. "I think Savannah really did have a nice time. I believe she felt very grown-up. And she was right about one thing—it would have been a mistake to have you at that party. You would have been totally out of place."

Grady relaxed. "I'm sure she was glad you were there with her."

Maybe too glad, Alexis thought, realizing the two of them

were getting as close as mother and daughter. That would be a problem if Grady ever decided to ease her out of Savannah's life…. The last thing she wanted was to break this precious little girl's heart.

Grady saw through her defenses to her distress. "Anything else happen?" he asked gently.

Alexis went to get her purse from the table on the foyer, where she'd left it. Returning, she gave Grady the computer-generated reminder. "I ran into the mother in charge of the uniforms for next year. Apparently, she has been e-mailing and telephoning you to try and get Savannah's measurements?"

Grady put the name and phone number on his desk. "I'm going to contact the uniform coordinator on Friday, at the same time I notify the school that Savannah won't be attending Miss Chilton's Academy for Young Women next year. I didn't want to say anything before graduation. Figured it would create too much of a stir."

Alexis couldn't blame him for that. Savannah had been through enough where Principal Jordan and the mean girls in her class were concerned. She put her purse aside and went back to the sofa, perching on the arm to face Grady. "When are you going to tell Savannah she's switching schools?"

Grady's glance traced the curve of Alexis's stocking-clad knee before returning to her face. "While we're in Laramie, visiting family during the upcoming holiday. I'm going to take her over and show her where I went to elementary school and explain to her that her new school will be just like that."

Alexis could tell he'd given this a lot of thought. "I think she'll be a lot happier in a coed school."

"I do, too." Grady clamped a hand on Alexis's wrist and tugged her down onto the cushion next to him. "Anything else happen?"

Should she tell him? Alexis wondered, straightening her skirt. Heaven knew she didn't want Grady finding out about the mini-contretemps any other way.... "Kit Peterson pulled me aside to let me know that she is not happy with me."

Grady's brow furrowed. "How come?"

Another long story she would rather not have to relate. "Kit sent a friend—Zoe Borden—to my office and had Zoe request me as matchmaker, thinking that she could just ask for a date with you and I would arrange it."

Grady shook his head in irritation. "Kit already tried to set us up last year, right after Zoe separated from her third husband. I told Kit I wasn't interested."

"Well, they're both hoping that will change, now that Zoe is divorced."

"The only woman," Grady said, drawing Alexis close enough for a passionate, lingering kiss, "I'm interested in is you."

"Yes, well..." Forcing herself to remain as composed as she needed to be, Alexis extricated herself from the comfort of Grady's arms, stood and began to pace the length of the living room. "The news is also out that I've been staying here the past couple of nights."

Grady stood, too. "How would they know that?" he demanded.

"Savannah told everyone I was sleeping here."

"In the guest room," Grady corrected, not impressed by the gossip of that particular tale.

Aware what thin ice she was already on, as far as her request for promotion at her company was concerned, Alexis pressed her lips together. "Savannah may have left that detail out."

Grady closed the distance between them, lifted his arms and cupped her shoulders in his palms. "I'm sorry."

Alexis did her best to ignore the warmth of his touch, transmitting through to her skin. "It's all right." She swallowed, wishing she wasn't so emotionally involved. She feigned nonchalance. "I appreciate the hospitality you've shown me the past few days, and I set Kit straight on the matter, so..."

For the first time, Grady looked upset. "Kit's the one who..."

"Let that little detail slip?" Alexis flushed, despite herself. "Yes. She accused me of setting my sights on you from the beginning."

He used the leverage of his grip to bring her ever closer. "We both know that isn't true. What's happened between us..."

Just once, Alexis wished Grady would say or do something to indicate he was beginning to love her as much as she loved him. "Just happened, I know."

When he spoke, his voice was matter-of-fact but kind. "Are you okay with this?"

On the surface...? Sure. Words couldn't hurt her. Privately, Alexis wasn't certain. Like it or not, Kit's spiteful assertion that she was nothing more than a rebound fling to Grady had hit home. Alexis wanted to think it wasn't true. She wanted to believe she and Grady were on the road to something real and lasting and true. But what if they weren't? What if Kit's prediction was correct, that her fling with Grady was all she would ever have?

He was still waiting for an answer.

"I'm fine," Alexis fibbed, working hard to make her expression just as inscrutable as his. "I'm just really tired." She put up a hand, staving off further conversation, freeing herself from his grip. "I think I'll hit the sack early."

Clearly disappointed, he stepped back, too, then inquired softly, "You're sure you don't want to hang out for a while, watch some television?"

Alexis declined his offer with a shake of her head and moved toward the hall. "Thanks, but no."

LONG AFTER ALEXIS HAD departed, Grady couldn't shake the feeling that something more was wrong, something Alexis had yet to reveal. He wondered if her pensive mood had anything to do with the promotion she was still waiting to hear about. Had she received the Galveston job, and had yet to tell him she would soon be moving? Or had she lost the opportunity—because he had dominated her time—and then quit the matchmaking service entirely?

Unfortunately, she was already in bed for the night. By the time she emerged from her room the next morning, showered and dressed, Savannah was up and his parents had arrived.

The five of them drove to the girls' academy together. Then they all watched with pride as Savannah walked up to receive her diploma, a child-size white satin graduation cap with tassel on her head. As she shook Principal Jordan's hand, she turned and smiled for the camera. With a lump in his throat the size of a walnut, Grady snapped the photo, along with the event photographer, then smiled and waved. His daughter waved back, her attention turning to the other guests in their party. Grady couldn't say he was surprised to see his parents were all choked up, too. They burst with pride at every milestone their five offspring took, and now that pride extended to their only grandchild.

What cemented the lump in his throat was the sight of Alexis in the audience, looking as proud—and emotional—as every mother there.

Grady had half expected that. He knew Alexis loved Savannah, and that his daughter loved her back.

What Grady hadn't counted on was the surprising depth

of his own feelings, the fact he was experiencing emotions he had never expected or wanted to be subjected to again.

Was it possible? he wondered. Could it be…?

There was no time to contemplate further. Another child was taking the stage and he was in the way. Surreptitiously blinking back the moisture in his eyes, he waved at Savannah one more time, then sneaked back down the aisle and resumed his seat next to his family.

"You know," Wade told Savannah later, over their celebratory graduation lunch downtown, "you are our first grandchild to graduate from kindergarten."

Savannah giggled. "Granddad. I'm your only grandchild."

"For right now," Josie pointed out with a smile. "But we have hopes that some more little darlin's will be joining our family very soon." She looked pointedly at her son.

Grady swore silently to himself. His mother had a matchmaking gleam in her eye. And while he couldn't say his thoughts weren't ambling along the same trail, he did not want his mother saying or doing anything that would alarm an already skittish Alexis, to the point she exited from his life.

Thankfully, his dad stepped in to take his wife's hand. "Hold on there, sweetheart. For that to happen somebody's got to fall in love and get married first," Wade said. Then his father turned and looked at Grady expectantly, the very same gleam in his eyes.

Alexis flushed bright pink and dropped her gaze to her plate.

"Just to be clear…they're not talking about us," Grady rushed to reassure her, in an effort to alleviate some of the familial pressure. He glared at his folks, letting them know it was past time to back off. Sure, they might have figured out what Alexis had yet to discern—that he was more emotionally available than he had realized. But that didn't mean they had to spill the beans.

Telling Alexis that he was a helluva lot more ready for commitment than he had figured was his business. Not theirs.

Grady continued the face-saving explanation of his parents' matchmaking behavior. "They're talking about my four younger brothers."

His folks, getting the hint at long last, just smiled and nodded amiably.

"Speaking of fun," his mother said finally, turning to Savannah, "your granddad and I are headed back to our ranch near Laramie this very afternoon. We're going to get ready for our big Fourth of July picnic and barbecue. And guess what? We could use an assistant. Do you know any big girls of, say, five or so, who might be able to help us?"

"IT WAS NICE OF your parents to take Savannah for a few days," Alexis said a few hours later, after the trio had left.

Grady walked into his study. He turned off his cell phone and set it on his desk, then turned back to her. "They try to give me a break from parenting every month or two. Usually it's pretty lonely around here with Savannah gone. But I have to say..." He stepped toward Alexis and wrapped his hands around her waist "...I'm looking forward to the time alone with you."

She pulled away from him, or attempted to, anyway. He had a pretty good hold on her. "Grady, I—I think we need to talk."

He flattened his hands over her spine, brought her even closer and lowered his head. "First things first," he murmured.

As always, the resistance in her began to fade within the first couple seconds of their kiss. Her body softening, she opened her mouth to the insistent pressure of his, and pulled him seductively closer. A thrill shot through him at the heady sensation of her breasts crushed against his chest. Blood rushed to his groin. Need and want combined.

He lifted her onto the edge of his desk. She caught her breath as he pushed her skirt up and stepped between her spread thighs. Still kissing her, he divested her of the jacket and began working on the single button of her silk blouse at the nape of her neck.

She gave a soft murmur of ascent and lifted her arms as he eased the fabric over her head. It fell in a puddle on his desk, followed swiftly by her bra. Cupping her breasts with his hands, he took her mouth once again. Moaning, she tightened her grip on him, her body arching. And Grady felt everything he had ever wanted, everything he had ever needed, flooding back into his life.

She was something, this woman.

Alexis made him want to risk again, want to love and live, and count his blessings—not just at times like now, but all the time. She made him want to create a family with the three of them. And she dared him to dream of more than he'd ever thought possible.

For the first time, he could imagine himself having more kids.

Having a wife…

And a relationship that lasted not just until fate cruelly intervened, but for the rest of his life…

For the first time, he could envision a future.

And that future centered around Alexis.

ALEXIS DIDN'T KNOW HOW IT happened, how it always happened. One minute she'd made up her mind to do the cautious thing and take a step back. The next, Grady would be gazing at her, and that have-to-have-you-right-now look of his would translate into a touch, and then a kiss, and the next thing she knew she'd be half-naked and wanting him naked, too.

She moaned low in her throat as the kiss deepened intimately. He kissed her cheek, her chin, her throat, and when his lips dropped even lower, she knew it was all over.

There would be no resisting him—no resisting this. No wait-and-see-if-it-all-worked-out before she got herself in any deeper. She was already in as far as she was going to go. Already in love with him. Already wanting a future that included Grady and Savannah and all the things she'd feared were out of her reach forever…

Her skirt came off. So did his shirt and pants….

Naked, they made it as far as the leather wing reading chair.

He sank into it. She dropped onto him, her head beginning to buzz, as their lips met in a kiss that was hot and hard and sweet. Aroused to distraction, she made a cradle of her hips, easing him into it, every inch of her body beginning to fuse to his. She hung on to that feeling, hung on to him, hands and lips exploring each other's bodies. And then there was no more thinking, no more waiting, nothing but the sheer pleasure of their joining. They clung together afterward, trembling and breathless. Knowing, as good as it had been, that it wasn't over yet.

Aware of how she never wanted to be away from him again, she let him lead her upstairs to his bed. Let him coax her between the sheets and back in his arms again, until she felt the now familiar hardness pressing against her. She knew if she did not extricate herself promptly, she would only fall deeper in love, in lust. But when he slid down, parted her knees and buried his face between her thighs, all thoughts of caution fled.

She could get hurt, handing her heart and soul to him like this. This could only be a rebound for him. But even if it was, had anything ever felt this glorious?

Alexis had never imagined lovemaking could be so tender and hot, uninhibited and fulfilling. Was it any wonder that she caught his head in her hands and brought him closer, thrilled at each expert caress of his tongue? Or found endless ways to pleasure him to oblivion, too? Or that in the end they would end up together again, hips locked, rocking in rhythm. His body felt so warm and strong and good; his weight made her feel so safe, his lips and hands so loved. Every time he moved to possess her, he thrust more deeply home.

Before long, she was teetering on the brink, falling, rising, spiraling into bliss… And then the room grew silent once more, their bodies entwined, her whole being at peace.

ALEXIS WOKE TO THE faraway ringing of her cell phone, discerning by the type of buzzing that it was the office. A glance at the bedside clock told her it was almost five in the afternoon. She groaned, burying her head in the pillow. "This is beginning to be a ritual," she lamented in a muffled voice. "Make love with you…" recklessly and passionately "…and get called by work."

Grady drew her back against him. He wrapped both arms around her and nuzzled the side of her neck. "Don't get it."

Temptation swirled through her, as potent as having him next to her. "I have to." Sighing, she disentangled herself and threw on Grady's robe. "Holly Anne wanted to tell me about the Galveston job."

"Well?" he said when she had finished her conversation and rejoined him in the master bedroom.

Trying hard not to notice how sexy Grady looked, lying back among the rumpled sheets, Alexis dropped the stack of their discarded clothing she had brought upstairs with her on the bench at the end of the bed. Her emotions awhirl, she perched on the mattress, facing him. "I didn't get it."

His expression immediately contrite, Grady sat up. "I'm sorry."

"I am, too, about the money. It would have been nice to be able to pay off my debt a lot faster, get a bit bigger place." She sighed, determined to be as honest with him as she was with herself. "But on the other hand, I really don't want to move to Galveston right now. Not anymore."

He studied her, his expression inscrutable. "What's changed?" he asked gently.

Why pretend she wasn't completely in love with him? Surely he had to have some idea.... Surveying him just as carefully, she said lightly, "You even have to ask?"

Grady pulled her back into his arms. He kissed her warmly, then lounged against the headboard, holding her close. "I feel bad," he told her bluntly. "You lost that job because of me."

"And me." Alexis took credit where credit was due. "I didn't have to get so besotted by you."

He stroked a hand over her hair. "But you did," he murmured in her ear, "which is why I'm thinking we should do something about it."

Alexis's heart began to pound. Suddenly, she couldn't get her breath. "Like what, exactly?"

He ran a hand up and down her back. "Like make it easier for you to pay off your debts faster—and have a nice place to live. And since you won't accept my financial help—"

Alexis's spine stiffened at the idea of being anyone's charity case. "You're right," she said stubbornly. "I will not!"

Grady seemed to be prepared for that. And she supposed, knowing her as he did, he probably was.

His lips turned up in a casual smile. "How about something more neighborly, then?"

She tensed again. Sensing a trap, she asked cautiously, "Like what?"

Without warning, his eyes turned serious. "Like you give up your apartment and move in with me and Savannah permanently."

Chapter Fourteen

Grady looked at Alexis. The stunned expression on her face was not the reaction he had been hoping for. It didn't mean all was lost, just that he had to have a better pitch.

After all, he had the McCabe and the Corbett-Wyatt genes. He knew how to finesse a situation that would leave everyone not only richer, but much happier to boot.

"You're here all the time, anyway. We have a guest room that stands empty. Savannah adores you and she's been longing for a mommy in her life. You've met that need." Feeling her sink even farther away from him, Grady flashed a winning smile. "I love having you around, too."

She started to turn away, but he caught her hands and drew her back. "I love making love with you, being with you," he told her sincerely.

She didn't respond.

He tried again. "I want to help. I want to be part of your life."

Still nothing.

"I want you to be part of ours." *Just the way you have been.* "I want us to be—"

"Like family?" Alexis interrupted, not looking all that pleased.

Well, no, Grady thought, that wasn't what he wanted. He wanted them to *be* family. But, figuring that wasn't what she wanted to hear—at least not this soon in their relationship—Grady said the word he expected she wanted. "Sure."

She let go of his hands as swiftly as if he had burned her. And this time she did turn away, looking thoroughly ticked off. "I don't think so." She pushed the words through gritted teeth, snatched up the scattered pieces of clothing she had worn to Savannah's graduation, and headed into the master bathroom.

Grady followed and planted himself in the doorway, feeling as if he were squaring off with a bear that had caught its paw in a trap. "You're mad?"

She whirled, sending a wave of her perfume drifting his way. "Gee…you think?"

Not giving him a chance to answer, she tossed her clothing on the marble counter and slammed the bathroom door in his face. Grady heard the swish of cloth on the other side. He leaned against the doorframe, trying not to envision the splendid beauty of her nakedness. "Okay. So maybe it's a little soon to be asking you to move in with us."

The silence was broken only by the rasp of a zipper.

"But it's what I want," Grady continued, over more rustling cloth. "I'm not going to lie about that."

The door swung open. Alexis marched out, still buttoning the jacket of her suit. "I'm not going to lie, either. It's not what I want."

He watched her hunt around for her sling-back heels. "I thought—"

"I know." She sat down on the bed to put on her shoes, her skirt hiking up well past her knees. "You had every reason to come to that conclusion." Finished, she stood. "I've behaved like a fool. But no more."

"Alexis—"

She spun around to face him, tears glimmering in her eyes. "I told you when we first met, Grady. I'm tired of only living half a life." She held up her hand before he could interrupt. "I don't want to do that anymore. I don't *want* to settle for friendship when I might have the kind of love I had with my husband."

Grady stared at her, aghast. How could he have been so wrong? So sure she mirrored the way he felt, deep inside? He swallowed, realizing his whole world was crashing down around him, without warning, once again. Fighting to keep a tight rein on his emotions, he swallowed. "You're saying that what I am offering isn't enough?"

It was her turn to look unbearably disappointed. Alexis sighed, swept her hands through her tousled hair and sadly met his eyes. "I'm saying what I've said all along, Grady. I'm tired of living a diminished life. No one knows how much time they have here on earth, but while I'm here, I want it all. And until I get it, I'd rather be alone."

"DADDY, IS ALEXIS STILL looking for a new mommy for me?" Savannah asked three days later, as they walked onto the front porch at his parents' ranch.

Setting down the huge basket of corn his mother had asked him to shuck, Grady took a seat on the cushioned wicker settee. "Um, no, honey, she's not," he drawled as the scents of mesquite and slow-roasting barbecue filled the manicured yard. "I told her it probably wasn't the right time for me to start dating again."

In the distance, his dad and some of his brothers worked on setting up the portable dance floor, while two more minded the wood-fueled smokers.

"That's good." Savannah settled next to him and accepted

an ear of corn. She peeled off one green leaf, then another, revealing the layer of cornsilk underneath.

"How come?" Grady asked, husking an ear with two swift pulls.

"Because I don't want a new mommy," Savannah said, serious as could be. "I just want Alexis."

So did Grady. "I know you do, honey."

"How come we haven't seen her?"

"She's been really busy," he fibbed, not about to tell his daughter the woman she wanted in her life was no longer going to be there.

It was hard enough for him to accept. How could he ask Savannah to do the same?

"Is Alexis coming here to eat barbecue and see the fireworks with us?" Savannah struggled to pick the silk off the kernels.

"No." Grady picked up another ear and methodically shucked it, too.

His daughter looked as sad and disappointed as Grady felt. Her lower lip trembled and tears shone in her eyes. "Doesn't she like Laramie?"

Irritated with himself for bringing a woman into their lives, only to have the relationship end as unfairly as his marriage had, Grady worked to spare his daughter's feelings once again. "I'm sure she would like Laramie just fine, if she'd ever been here."

Savannah dropped her shucked ear into the bowl of cleaned cobs and grabbed another. "Then why won't she come to our Fourth of July party?"

Maybe it was time to be a little more open. "I think she might be mad at me," he admitted finally.

His daughter looked as if she found that hard to believe. "Why?"

Discovering it was more difficult to curtail his emotions with every second that passed, Grady exhaled. "I'm not sure."

Savannah narrowed her eyes. She wasn't buying that for one red-hot second.

"Okay, maybe I have an idea," Grady allowed. "I think I might have rushed her." Either that or Alexis didn't see herself ever falling in love with him, and that wasn't an idea he wanted to wrap his mind around. He didn't want to think he'd been nothing more than a fling to her....

Savannah blinked. "What does that mean?"

It means, Grady thought, *I shouldn't have asked Alexis to move in, when love isn't in the cards for us—at least as far as she's concerned.* The only thing she apparently had wanted from him was temporary passion. The kind that took someone off the bench and put him or her back in the game.

Which was why, he realized way too late, he should have followed his instincts and never gotten off the bench in the first place. He'd been right to think that lightning only strikes once in a lifetime. Correct to feel that the odds of him falling for a woman who would in turn, fall for him were astronomically against it. He hadn't wanted to be hurt again or feel mind-numbing loss. Yet here he was, feeling worse than if he had just remained alone and celibate for the rest of his life. What kind of fool did that make him? What kind of father?

"Daddy?" Savannah said, sounding a little less hurt and a lot more reasonable.

Unable to quell his sadness, Grady looked down at her. "What, pumpkin?"

His five-year-old daughter gave him the stern but loving look he always gave her when he reprimanded her. "I think you should just say you're sorry. Then Alexis won't be mad at you anymore."

Had the situation not been so completely disillusioning, her dictum would have been funny. "Honey, I wish it was that easy. I really do."

Savannah stamped her foot. "But, Daddy, you always tell me—"

"Not in this case."

She slumped in her seat, looking as if her heart would break. As if she'd almost had everything she ever wanted, only to have it cruelly snatched away.

Unfortunately, Grady knew exactly how his little girl felt.

ALEXIS WAS IN THE OFFICE, catching up on work, when her phone rang. Wondering who it could be, since she hadn't told anyone she was spending the holiday alone, she picked up.

"You're a hard woman to track down," Josie McCabe said.

"Sorry." Alexis had turned off her cell. She hadn't wanted to think about the calls she wouldn't be getting from Josie's son. "I've been catching up on a lot of work." Or trying to. She hadn't actually been getting a lot done.

"Honey," the woman chided. "On a holiday?"

Alexis felt a pensive smile coaxed from her lips. If she were in the market for a mom to replace the one she'd lost, she wouldn't mind it being Josie McCabe. But Josie couldn't be her mom unless she was connected to Grady.

"I think I have an idea why you're calling," Alexis said.

"Because you broke my son's heart?" Josie interrupted, with her customary gentleness.

Alexis was a little taken aback. "For me to break Grady's heart, he would have to love me first," she corrected.

Josie paused, then asked incredulously, "Who says he doesn't?"

Who else? "Grady!"

"He said that?" Josie gasped.

Alexis lifted her shoulders in a listless shrug and rocked back in her chair. "It was more what he *didn't* say."

His mother harrumphed. "That sounds like a McCabe male. Thinking it's all obvious and therefore there's no reason to state the obvious."

That made sense. Sort of. Alexis sat forward slightly and rubbed her temples. "What is the obvious?"

Josie paused again. "Don't you think you should be asking Grady that?"

Alexis ignored the gentle teasing in the woman's voice. She traced a random pattern on her desk with her fingertip. "I don't think we're speaking right now."

"And whose decision was that?" Josie demanded.

Good question.

"Look," she continued, her exasperation clear. "I don't know exactly what happened between the two of you. My son is not telling me anything, as usual. I do know what I saw when you were together. And I know what I see today when you're not with each other. He needs you, Alexis, and unless I'm mistaken, you need him, too."

The truth of the assessment hit home. Tears blurred Alexis's vision. Although the selfish part of her felt she loved Grady enough for both of them, she knew from her work as a matchmaker that one-sided love rarely worked out long term. In those situations, someone always got hurt. And in this situation, it wouldn't be just her and Grady—Savannah would get hurt, too. Alexis couldn't bear that, any more than she could bear the thought of a life without Grady and the little girl she had come to love as her very own.

She didn't want to shortchange either of them. Need wasn't love. Grady deserved to love and be loved as much as she did. "Believe me, I wish you were right, but it's not that simple," she protested in a choked voice, feeling as if her heart was breaking all over again.

She wanted Grady—and Savannah—to have everything they deserved.

"Honey, it's as simple as you want it to be. Follow your feelings. Get in the car and drive to Laramie. Spend the holiday with us."

"Grady—"

"Will be happy to see you."

FINDING THE MCCABES' RANCH outside Laramie was the easy part. Getting up the nerve to get out of her car and go find Wade and Josie's eldest son was a lot harder. What if Grady didn't want her there? He hadn't invited her to the party. On the other hand, if she didn't take some risk, she'd never be happy again. And she so much wanted to be happy.

Alexis drew a deep, bolstering breath, opened the car door and got out.

Over the roof of the car, she saw a familiar figure striding toward her. It was Grady. Not in the city clothes she usually saw him in, but in jeans, boots and a white Western shirt. He had a straw hat slanted low over his brow. Although she couldn't see his eyes, she *could* see the serious slant of his mouth. His lips were thinned, his jaw set in the same grim don't-mess-with-a-McCabe tilt she had witnessed the other night, when she'd walked out on him.

Her spirits rose and then sank, then rose again.

And suddenly he was bypassing the three-dozen vehicles already parked on the lawn, on either side of the long elegant drive. Quickly rounding the back of her car, he came to stand beside her. In the distance, Alexis could hear the sounds of a party. Lively music, laughter, shrieking children, the raucous splashes of people jumping into a swimming pool. But here in the quickly diminishing light, there were only the two of them. Only this moment in time. Maybe even only this chance.

Alexis looked up at him, heart in her throat, her emotions on the line. She felt her eyes brim with tears. It was time to take a risk. Way past time. "About moving in with you?" she said simply, her gaze on his face. "My answer is yes."

Grady stared at her, undecipherable emotion flickering in his eyes.

Silence strung out between them.

Finally, he grimaced and said, with what sounded very much like a mixture of gratitude and regret, "I don't think it's a good idea."

Something crashed inside her once again.

He took her hand. Their fingers twined and he stared down at the place where their palms interlocked. Finally, he looked back up again. "You deserve better."

Suddenly, the happy future she'd once thought would never be hers seemed almost within reach. "I don't want better," she blurted. "I want…you, Grady. Only you."

He grinned and he tugged her closer, the affection she had been craving visible in his eyes. "Maybe you don't want better, but you should have it," he told her, pausing to take her chin in hand and deliver a soft, searing kiss that turned her life upside down once again. Drawing back slightly, he gently caressed her face with the flat of his palm. "You should have everything that's been missing from your life the last few years. Romance, passion, fun, excitement, tenderness. And most of all," he told her solemnly, "you should have a once-in-a-lifetime love. You deserve that, Alexis, and so much more. And so do I. Which is why," he continued hoarsely, "I think we should take a step back."

"A step back." Alexis didn't know why she was repeating his statement. She had understood very well what he'd just said. She just hadn't wanted to hear it. "Okay then..." She started to turn away.

He held fast, refusing to release the grip he had on her hand.

"I know I screwed up," he confessed, his eyes on her face. "I know I pushed you too hard, too fast. I was selfish, but I couldn't help it. I love you, Alexis. I love you with all my heart."

A hiccup caught in her throat. The tears she'd been holding back flowed, full force. "Oh Grady, I love you, too." Alexis wreathed her arms about his neck. They kissed, long and slow...soft and sweet. "I just said no because I thought you didn't love me!"

He paused, taking that in, then grasped her upper arms. "I thought you walked away because you didn't think you could ever love me."

Joy began to spiral through her. "Well, I guess we were wrong about that," Alexis said, releasing a tremulous sigh.

"Seems so." Happiness radiating from him, he bent his head and delivered another tender kiss.

"So about your offer..." Alexis said between kisses.

"We're not moving in together," Grady announced firmly. "Not just as friends and lovers, anyway." His voice dropped. "What we have is far too special for that."

This, she thought, sounded serious. But she had come to some important conclusions, too. "Life is short, Grady. Sometimes too short. I've waited a lifetime to feel this way again. I don't want to miss a single second of it, due to some arbitrary time frame everyone else thinks we should adhere to."

"I was hoping you'd feel that way…." Grinning, he reached into his pocket and withdrew a velvet box, which he pressed into her palm. She opened it with shaking hands. Inside was a beautiful platinum solitaire engagement ring, with tiny diamonds all around the band. It was the most beautiful ring she had ever seen, just perfect for her in so many ways.

As firecrackers shot off in the distance, illuminating the sky, Grady dropped to one knee and looked up at her, love shining in his eyes. "Which is why I'm asking if you'll do me the honor of saying you'll be wife."

Epilogue

Three months later…

Savannah bounced up and down with excitement. "I knew we'd get to wear flowers in our hair!"

Alexis secured the last pin, holding the wreath in place, then stepped back to survey her handiwork. Savannah looked precious in a pale blue silk-flower girl dress, white tights and white patent leather Mary Janes.

"How's it going in here?" Grady slipped in the guest bedroom door.

"Daddy!" Savannah shrieked. "You're not supposed to see us yet!"

He grinned, unrepentant. "I won't tell if you won't."

His daughter surveyed him, deciding.

"It's okay," Alexis said, soothing the little girl who would soon officially be her daughter. "I asked Daddy to come in so the three of us could have a moment alone before we go downstairs to get married."

They had decided to wait to get married until Savannah was nicely settled in her new school, which she now was. In the meantime, the three of them had spent every evening together, savoring each other's company and making plans. And Alexis had approached her job as a matchmaker at ForeverLove.com with new energy and commitment, counseling her clients not to settle for anything less than real, lasting love, because, as she and Grady could attest, a love like theirs was worth waiting for.

Now, finally, after counting down the days until she and Grady were to be wed in his home, with only a few close friends and family present, that day had finally arrived. The downstairs was filled with flowers. A harp and flute duo were at the ready. Caterers were setting up a reception beneath a tent in the back yard. The minister had arrived. And Savannah was still considering whether her dad should be allowed to see them.

"I wanted to get a good look at my girls before we went to join everyone else." Grady picked up the explanation where Alexis had left off. He held out his arms and waited.

Savannah did a princess pirouette.

"Beautiful!" Grady said, giving his little girl a hug. He gestured to Alexis. "Your turn."

She did a pirouette, too.

Savannah sighed, completely enthralled. "You look really pretty," she declared.

Grady's eyes glowed. "Absolutely gorgeous," he agreed.

Alexis *felt* stunning, in the strapless, ivory silk gown. She gave Grady a slow once-over. He looked very handsome in a charcoal-gray tuxedo. "You're pretty handsome, too."

"Very handsome," Savannah agreed. Already bored with the conversation, she sprinted toward the door. "I'm going to find my flower basket!"

Once again Alexis and Grady were alone. Contentment flowed, and their future beckoned, as bright and dazzling as the diamond sparkling on Alexis's left hand.

"Have I told you lately," he murmured, taking her in his arms and holding her close, "how happy you've made me?"

"All the time." Alexis drank in the clean, familiar scent of him. "And for the record, you've made me incredibly happy, too." They kissed slowly and sweetly.

Downstairs, the music started. Savannah clattered back up the stairs. Reluctantly, bride and groom moved apart.

"Then there's only one thing to do," Grady drawled as his daughter burst through the door, petals from the flower basket already spraying every which way. "Let's get married."

"Yes!" Savannah shouted. "And live happily ever after!"

"Sounds good to me." Alexis paused to kiss both of them.

So they did.

* * * * *

Watch out for Cathy Gillen Thacker's upcoming miniseries starring Grady McCabe's friends—
THE LONE STAR DADS CLUB—
beginning October 2009.

ALEXANDROS KAREDES, SNOW DUSTING the shoulders of his leather jacket and glittering like jewels in his dark hair, stood at the door. Maria felt the blood drain from her head.

"Good evening, Ms. Santos."

His voice was as she remembered it. Deep. Husky. Perfect English, but with the faintest hint of a Greek accent. And cold, as cold as it had been that awful morning she would never forget, when he'd accused her of horrible things, called her terrible names....

"Aren't you going to ask me in?"

She fought for composure. Last time they'd faced each other, they'd been on his turf. Now they were on hers. She was in command here, and that meant everything.

"There's a sign on the door downstairs," she said, her tone every bit as frigid as his. "It says, 'No soliciting or vagrants.'"

His lips drew back in a wolfish grin. "Very amusing."

"What do you want, Prince Alexandros?"

A tight smile eased across his mouth and it killed her that even now, knowing he was a vicious, arrogant man, she couldn't help but notice what a handsome mouth it was. Chiseled.

Generous. Beautiful, like the rest of him, which made him living proof that beauty could, indeed, be only skin deep.

"Such formality, Maria. You were hardly so proper the last time we were together."

She knew his choice of words was deliberate. She felt her face heat; she couldn't help that but she damned well didn't have to let him lure her into a verbal sparring match.

"I'll ask you once more, your highness. What do you want?"

"Ask me in and I'll tell you."

"I have no intention of asking you in. Tell me why you're here or don't. It's your choice, just as it will be my choice to shut the door in your face."

He laughed. It infuriated her but she could hardly blame him. He was tall—six two, six three—and though he stood with one shoulder leaning against the door frame, hands tucked casually into the pockets of the jacket, his pose was deceptive. He was strong, with the leanly muscled body of a well-trained athlete.

She remembered his body with painful clarity. The feel of him under her hands. The power of him moving over her. The taste of him on her tongue.

Suddenly, he straightened, his laughter gone. "I have not come this distance to stand in your doorway," he said coldly, "and I am not going to leave until I am ready to do so. I suggest you stand aside and stop behaving like a petulant child."

A petulant child? Was that what he thought? This man who had spent hours making love to her and had then accused her of—of trading her body for profit?

Except it had not been love, it had been sex. And the sooner she got rid of him, the better.

She let go of the doorknob and stepped aside. "You have five minutes."

He strolled past her, bringing cold air and the scent of the night with him. She swung toward him, arms folded. He reached past her, pushed the door closed, then folded his arms, too. She wanted to open the door again but she'd be damned if she was going to get into a who's-in-charge-here argument with him. She was in charge, and he would surely see a tussle over the ground rules as a sign of weakness.

Instead, she looked past him at the big clock above her work table.

"Ten seconds gone," she said briskly. "You're wasting time, your highness."

"What I have to say will take longer than five minutes."

"Then you'll just have to learn to economize. More than five minutes, I'll call the police."

Instantly, his hand was wrapped around her wrist. He tugged her toward him, his dark-chocolate eyes almost black with anger.

"You do that and I'll tell every tabloid shark I can contact about how Maria Santos tried to buy a five-hundred-thousand-dollar commission by seducing a prince." He smiled thinly. "They'll lap it up."

* * * * *

What will it take for this billionaire prince to realize he's falling in love with his mistress…?
Look for
BILLIONAIRE PRINCE, PREGNANT MISTRESS
by Sandra Marton.
Available July 2009 from Harlequin Presents®.

Tell
HARLEQUIN

Stay up-to-date on all your romance reading news!

The Inside Romance newsletter is a **FREE** quarterly newsletter highlighting our upcoming series releases and promotions!

Go to
eHarlequin.com/InsideRomance
or e-mail us at
InsideRomance@Harlequin.com
to sign up to receive
your FREE newsletter today!

You can also subscribe by writing to us at: HARLEQUIN BOOKS
Attention: Customer Service Department
P.O. Box 9057, Buffalo, NY 14269-9057

Please allow 4-6 weeks for delivery of the first issue by mail.

IRNBPA0109